A BALANCED APOCALYPSE

BOOK I OF THE VOID

BRADLEY RITO

ISBN: 978-1-957203-68-3 (sc)
ISBN: 978-1-957203-69-0 (hc)
ISBN: 978-1-957203-70-6 (e)

Because of the dynamic nature of the Internet, any web addresses or links contained in this book may have changed since publication and may no longer be valid. The views expressed in this work are solely those of the author and do not necessarily reflect the views of the publisher, and the publisher hereby disclaims any responsibility for them.

THE EWINGS PUBLISHING

One Galleria Blvd., Suite 1900, Metairie, LA 70001
1-888-421-2397

CONTENTS

Prologue vii

1. Rising Heat 1
2. Washed Away 11
3. A Rocky Past 16
4. Rogue Gust 22
5. The Four as One 27
6. Revelation by Light 31
7. Not a Dream...35
8. Free at Last 40
9. Darkness Revealed 44
10. Making the Most of It....................................49
11. Path to Paradise...56
12. Put to the Test 60
13. Falling Away..69
14. On the Run 76
15. The Heart of a Star..82
16. The Return 89
17. The Next Steps...95
18. Rolling in the Deep......................................101
19. Wing-Beaten 106
20. Saharan Surprise 110
21. What's in a Dream 116
22. Descending to Hell.......................................121
23. The Black Apple 126
24. Día de la Muerte..135

25. Six Feet Down Under 145

26. Retribution 153

27. Desecration of Holiness 159

28. Making Amends 166

29. The Final Task 176

30. An Uninvited Guest 181

Epilogue 187

PROLOGUE

The Seals of the Apocalypse, the gates that sealed away a darkness greater than any known or ever to be known: I used to believe they didn't exist, that they were all a ploy faiths used to get more money and attract more followers. I even laughed at the men and women on street corners yelling at every passerby that the world was ending. I would have never, in my wildest dreams, thought any of them were right, nor that they didn't seal away an even greater darkness, but more on that later.

To start, one must first understand that Revelation was wrong about how the apocalypse would happen and that Genesis was wrong in regards to the story of Creation. There is a story before the story of Creation; the true reason Earth was made. All you need to know for now is that the Almighty God sealed away the greatest darkness of all behind many dimensions, each ruled by one of its members. The only one I wish to focus on for now is our dimension, ruled by Artaxerxes.

Artaxerxes (the one we on Earth call "Jesus") made our dimension in the beginning. He was not alone, though. The epitome of evil, Lucifer, an arch angel at the time, was also there. The seemingly endless oceans, the lush fields and forests brimming with life, the sound of the breeze's gentle whisper as it swept through the fields, it turned out to be too much for the arch angel. Seeing what Artaxerxes had made, Lucifer, being envious, wrathful, and prideful, attempted to destroy it all. For such graven sins, he was cast from Heaven, forever condemned to Earth for his betrayal. Upon his descent, he captured a young man named Dante, a faithful follower of Artaxerxes, and took over his mind. Seeing the destruction that followed, Artaxerxes deemed Dante and his followers "beyond saving," forever casting them from the ranks of "the saved." The story doesn't stop here though.

Artaxerxes knew this was the work of Lucifer. In response, He created four deities of the elements (fire, water, wind, and earth) to help Him find and lock away the Devil. Lucifer was found in Hell and, with the combined force of both Artaxerxes and the Four, was locked away where no one could reach him. The Four were also locked away, like Lucifer, to be awoken only if Lucifer awoke. The Devil's resting place was then locked by the Seven Seals.

Over time, the Seven Seals broke. Thanks to all the natural disasters, martyrdom, pestilence and famine, the war and death caused by nations, the Seven Deadly Sins running rampant throughout humanity, it bears no explaining that the seals stood no chance.

Nevertheless, Lucifer, after just 11,000 years, awoke, as did the souls of the Four. However, having slept for so long, they could not remember who or what they were. In spite of their amnesia, they found four unborn humans to serve as their hosts, four humans who later become the most unlikely candidates for being the saviors of all the Multiverse. It is here we start this chapter of our story.

RISING HEAT

The Sun crested over the horizon, spreading its light slowly forward across the thousands of miles of ocean before it reached the Correctional Facility for the Most Dangerous Young Adults, commonly referred to as simply "the facility." As the light reached the 20,000 ft.² island, it kissed the solar panels and sensors, turning off both the search lights and the overnight generators. The Sun made its way up the walls of the staff housing, the only building above ground. The front door to the building opened, a man in his mid-50s coming out as he fixed the baby-blue collar over his maroon sweater, then reaching down for his leather briefcase. He looked over at the sunrise, smiling at the prospect of the new day. He then proceeded to the entrance to the facility, riding the elevator down to the check-in 1,000 ft. below.

"Good morning, Dr. Leon," the guard at the front desk said, nodding with a smile. "A special request from the President for you." He lifted up a manila envelope, the word "confidential" stamped in big black letters across the front.

"And a good morning to you, too, Anatole," the doctor replied, nodding and reaching for the envelope to see what lay inside. After a couple moments of reading, he half-smiled. "So I get to deal with the good sergeant again today during my visits. Good to know." He then signed his name on the sign-in sheet and, waving, turned to the left. He walked around the circular tunnel, passing offices to doctors, various military personnel, surveillance rooms, and the cafeteria along the way. Having reached the other side, he turned to his left and proceeded down the hallway to his office. Upon reaching it, he told the guard at the door, "You may bring me my patients now."

As the guard reached the entrance to the hallway, he waved to the two guards at the door to the elevator to follow him and began the 1,000-ft. descent to the bottom. At the bottom rested cells made of an indestructible glass, each equipped with cameras, electric wiring, and knock-out gas dispensers. In them rested the four most-dangerous prisoners in the world (simply referred to as "the Four"), all of whom were under 24-hr. lockdown except when otherwise supervised.

Once the guards arrived, they pulled out their stun guns and full-body cuffs. They then approached a cell of a young man with a half-foot-high blood-red Mohawk, wearing a tattered gray jumpsuit. They punched in a code on his cell door, buzzing it open.

The three guards entered, stun guns drawn and one ready to chain the prisoner. "Get dressed, Duke," he said, tossing a cleaner gray uniform on top of him.

"Go to Hell," Duke spat at them, shoving the uniform off himself and rolling over on his bed so he wasn't facing them anymore. This was when one of them, he didn't see which one, yanked him into the air by his Mohawk and threw him to the ground.

"Get dressed!" one of them shouted again.

"Are you sure you really want to be doing that?" Duke spat as he got to his feet, his eyes beginning to glow a bright orange color and smoke emanating from his hands.

"Calm down!" the middle one asserted as he pointed a remote to the sprinklers lining Duke's cell. "Make this easy on yourself, Duke. Just get dressed and come with us."

Duke hesitated, hating them with every ounce of his being, but knowing he wouldn't be able to get back into bed while they were inside his cell. "Fine," he finally murmured. The glow dissipated from his eyes, the smoke disappeared, and he dressed himself in the cleaner uniform. Never once did he remove his gaze from the guards, though, distrust written across his face like an invisible tattoo.

The guard holding the chains tossed them to Duke. "You know the procedure. Make it snappy." By this time, Duke was dressed. He proceeded to put the shackles around his waist, ankles, and wrists, hating every minute of this humiliation. "Now step forward, slowly, with your hands open and palms facing us, and no funny business."

"Where are you taking me anyway?" he asked, reluctantly doing as he was instructed.

"You all have appointments with the psychologist today," one of them said, waving his gun in the direction of the elevator. "Plus, spitting on him during your last visit left a permanent scar on his chest. So, the Head of Security feels it's only proper you give him a formal apology in person. Finally, the Head of Security himself will be there for the purpose of updating your files."

"To Hell with your Boss. That bastard-"

"Shut your mouth right now!" one of the shorter guards howled, attempting to smack Duke in the back of the head with his taser.

"Chill," the tall one whispered, catching the gun before it hit Duke, "both of you." He turned back to Duke. "It's best if you not talk until we get to Dr. Leon's office."

"Fine," Duke said, stepping into the elevator, surrounded by the guards.

It was a silent ride up and walk to Dr. Leon's office, except for the rattling of his chains and the sound of the guards' boots against the concrete floors and cylindrical walls. "Now get in there," one of them said, pushing him into Dr. Leon's office. The guards shut the door behind him and lined the wall by the door, hands firmly grasping their drawn tasers.

"Well, Duke, it's good to see you again," Dr. Leon stated from his scarlet armchair, his legs crossed and his hands on his notepad, a smile on his face. He pulled a pen from behind his ear, his whitening hair neatly combed off to the side. "Please, have a seat." He gestured towards the couch to his right.

Duke walked over and sat down on the couch, facing away from the man. "I'm not apologizing if that's what you're expecting out of me," he sneered over his shoulder before looking away.

"Fine," the man sighed calmly. "You'll apologize when you're ready, I'm sure. Anyway, the Head of Security needs to update the President's files. So, I'll let him get to that first."

"Doesn't the President already have files on me?" Duke asked.

A tall man in an army uniform stepped forward, the leather gun holster with a custom-made pistol reflecting the lights overhead. The name on his uniform read "Russell." He gently brushed his hand over his nearly-bald scalp before reaching for the pen in his breast pocket. "Good morning, Duke."

"Good morning, Sergeant Asshole," Duke replied, spitting on the Sergeant's boots, which the Sergeant quickly kicked off before it fused to his foot.

The guards immediately cocked their guns, but put them down as they saw Russell waving them to back off. "I'll ignore that," he sighed, opening a folder and clipping it to his clipboard. "Anyway, we need a new file on you because the President requested all files be updated. I'm going to start with the general information. So, answer the questions to the best of your knowledge and we'll be done sooner." Clicking his pen, he asked, "Full name?"

"Duke Edward Vulcous."

"Date of birth?"

"March 10th, 2000."

"Okay, so age is eighteen. Hair color?"

"Red."

"Eye color?"

"Orange."

"Height?"

"5'10"."

"Weight?"

"145 pounds."

"Allergies?"

"None."

"Other medical conditions to be aware of?"

Duke turned his eyes in Russell's direction, but only saw a glimpse of the mountain of a man. "How do you want me to reply to that? My body temperature is over 110 degrees all the time, so constant fever?"

"It's normal for you though, but I'll make a note of it." He scratched away on his sheet for a few seconds before saying, "That's the basic info we need. Now we just need for you to give us your background story."

Duke turned and looked up at Russell, frowning. "I've given you my background story enough for you to be able to recite it back to me word-for-word. The memory still haunts me. I'm not giving it to you again." Duke looked back away.

"Duke," the sergeant sighed, clicking his pen, "you know why I'm asking for it and why I can't just put down what I remember. It's so the President can have an up-to-date hand-written copy of the backgrounds for you and the other three back in the cell block. There are still bodies unaccounted for and they're hoping any new information might surface in what you say this time. Plus, these are the orders I have been given. I can't argue with them."

"To Hell with you and your orders."

The sergeant then pulled out a case with eight syringes. Four of them were filled with a clear liquid, the other four with a thick bluish liquid. "I'm sure you don't even need to look up to know what I have in front of me. So, you can either tell me, or I can give you a shot of truth serum mixed with a mild sedative to make you cooperative. Which do you prefer?"

Duke looked over at Dr. Leon, frowning. "Doc, you know better than anyone how hard it is for me to think about what I did and my guilt regarding the situation. Isn't there anything you can do?"

Dr. Leon let out a heavy sigh. "You are right. You have more than proven your guilt in the previous session regarding what you did to your hometown, and constantly reopening those wounds more than is necessary does nothing for the healing process." Seeing the sergeant frowning out of the corner of his eye, he held up a finger to pause him. "However, orders are orders. These are orders direct from the president herself. My hands are tied. What I can offer in exchange is that, if you wish to talk about it with the rest of our session and work through whatever emotions it may stir up, my ears will be open to you, as they always are. How does that sound?" He put his finger down, watching as Duke clenched his fists, realizing that what Dr. Leon said was true.

"Fine," Duke spat, smacking the edge of the couch in front of him. "Close the case, though," he ordered, pointing at the sergeant.

"Fine," the sergeant said, closing the case and setting it behind him. He clicked his pen again. "Now, talk."

"I grew up in Grosse Ile, MI, an only child because my mother died during child birth. My father, in response to her death, took up alcohol in the hopes of forgetting his pain. It however never worked, because it only made him angrier with me, as he blamed me for her death, claiming she'd still be alive if I were never born. So, for the first sixteen years of my life, he would come home almost daily and physically assault me with anything from chairs, fists, kicks, empty bottles, anything he could get his hands on. Towards the end, he even started emptying live rounds on me if he was drunk enough. Luckily, he was a terrible shot, even when sober, and missed me. Eventually, I grew so tired of his abuse that my rage escalated into a literal wildfire. The whole island was set ablaze, yours truly being the only survivor. I escaped before the fire engines arrived."

"And where did you go?"

"I didn't get far. Cops picked me up across the river near a fast food joint. They asked me where I was going, where my family was. Feeling full of pride for what had happened, I told them outright they were dead, and that I was glad they were. They took me back to the station, and it wasn't long before they figured out I was the cause of around 10,000 deaths. I was kept in solitary at a maximum security prison until my trial, where I was found guilty of all charges. I was then moved back to the maximum security prison to waste away. Once this place was built, I was moved here. I've been here for two years now. Does that cover all your questions?" Duke looked up at Russell.

Russell clicked his pen and placed it back in his pocket. "That should do it." He closed the file and walked out of the room.

"Well," Dr. Leon inquired, picking up his own pen and paper, "shall we start off with how things have been going for you?"

"Do we ever not?" Duke retorted.

Dr. Leon snickered. "How right you are. I guess it's only traditional to start off that way, though."

Duke sighed, his head slumping. "I've been locked in various cells for three years. I'm about as good as anyone can expect, given my seclusion."

"I imagine such seclusion has not been easy, especially given your guilt for what you did. You never meant to cause the death and destruction you did, and yet you're locked away as if it were intentional. Rather than try to understand you and help you to control your anger, and therein your powers, they lock you away out of fear."

Duke looked at the doctor. "Does that mean you're afraid of me and think I should be locked up?"

"Not at all," Dr. Leon replied. "Admittedly, I may have been afraid at first, but that is because I did not know you. I did not understand what you and the other three have been through. Once I saw your humanity, your feelings behind your actions, I see you as being no different than any other person."

Duke sighed again. "Not that my humanity means anything. People will always fear me."

Dr. Leon paused, thinking about how best to respond. "People with power are always feared by someone. What's important to remember is that you've grown, and therefore so have your powers. So long as your temper remains in check, you may be able to use those powers for good someday, save lives rather than take them. Maybe then those who fear you will be those on the wrong side of the law. That raises the 'million-dollar question,' though: Have you been able to control it, like we've talked about?"

"Yes, I've prevented myself from burning the place down. Next question," Duke spat, sounding annoyed.

"Very well, very well. How has your appetite been?"

"I've eaten the crap they serve me if that's what you want to know."

"So, healthy enough. How about your relation with the other three?"

"With Aria, we don't talk, not that she talks much to begin with. With Virgil, we don't talk much either. We just sort of ignore each other. As for Lia, yeah, we talk, but it's to shout at each other mostly." He turned over and looked at Dr. Leon. "Nothing has changed from last time, so why are you asking me all these questions?"

"I need to ask you these questions so I can make thorough reports about the habits all four of you have."

Duke frowned, a slight annoyance entering his voice. "So we're just guinea pigs for you, things to test and study? Great to know we're playing a role, even if it is less than dirt." He turned back over to face the wall, listening to Dr. Leon jot something down on his paper.

"Have you been okay emotionally?"

Duke stopped dead in his thoughts when the doctor just came right out and asked that question, almost as if unaffected by his comment. "What? Where the hell did that come from?"

"What you just told me about being a 'guinea pig' or being 'less than dirt,' such negative self-perception is a sign of something far more serious, like depression, as is the lack of sociability." He took off his gold-rimmed glasses and set them on the table next to him. "As your psychologist, I have a great concern for your well-being, and I just want to make sure you're not contemplating any kind of rash decision, suicide or otherwise."

Duke looked over his shoulder, frowning. "You genuinely care for my well-being?" he asked, disbelieving.

"Well, yes. You are my patient, and I live to help those in need, like yourself. Whatever you have done in the past is in the past. Neither of us can change our actions, but we can learn from them, use them as a tool to build a better future for ourselves."

Duke looked at him for a little while longer, then turned away again. "That's bull crap. All you see when you see the four of us are walking dollar signs. By being the psychologist of the Four, it doesn't take a genius to figure out you are being paid at least three times as much as any normal psychologist just because of the risk factors involved. We're just walking paychecks to you and nothing more."

Dr. Leon's frown deepened, his heart aching from hearing such accusations. "Do you really see yourself as being so insignificant, Duke?"

"No, I don't see myself as insignificant. I see *you* as seeing *me* as insignificant."

Leon picked his glasses back up and started writing "projects self-perception on others" on his pad of paper again. "I see, a very interesting notion, even if it couldn't be less true."

Duke got up and walked towards the bookshelf which lined the wall he was facing. "Say what you want, doc, but you're only trying to convince *yourself* of the fact."

"Why are you pushing me away?" Dr. Leon asked.

"What do you mean?" Duke sneered.

"We were starting to make progress, even a connection, and now you are pulling away. I sense it's because you don't like to let people in, to see that you actually care. You put on this tough exterior to protect yourself from experiencing and confronting your own vulnerability. Like I said earlier, you are human, which means you hurt like all of us. It may not feel good to hurt, but that is a part of life." He paused, putting his pen down and staring over at the young man. "I also suspect you are trying to free yourself and forget your past. You want forget about your father and how he betrayed you, about how alone I imagine you felt among your peers. Correct me if I'm wrong, but I imagine you are resisting any urge you have of ever becoming like your father, hence the reason you avoid pain. If you avoid pain, you run no risk of being like him."

Images of his father flashed through his mind, and Duke's head slouched. "I will never be like him."

"Duke, your father did what he did out of a feeling of loneliness. I imagine your mother was his world, and then having her taken away like that left him dangerously depressed and feeling isolated from everyone and everything he knew. While you may not turn to alcohol as he did, I fear that, if you continue down this path of isolation, I have to wonder if it will make you any better than he was."

Duke froze in that split second, his fists clenching until they were a solid white. More memories of his father coming home drunk and beating him, shooting at him, and verbally abusing him in the worst possible ways came rushing through his mind. He turned around, eyes glowing, the heat he was producing softening the chains and allowing him to break free.

"Did you just say I'm like my father?" Duke snarled through gritted teeth, his glowing eyes glaring, the veins in his arms, neck, and hands bulging. The guards at the door hit a silent alarm and armed their stun guns. Duke hurled a stream of fire at them before they could pull the trigger.

Dr. Leon fell to the floor as the sprinklers burst on and the fire alarm when off. "I didn't say you are like your father," Leon corrected, stumbling towards the door to the bathroom. "I was saying if you continue to be so closed-minded and if you let your temper control you, not vice versa, you *may*, not *will*, *may* be no better than he was. Don't let your temper control you. Why don't we do some calming breaths, like I taught you?"

"We'll see how calm you can breathe when you're engulfed in flames!" Duke snapped, throwing a fireball at the psychologist, who quickly dove out of the way, the fireball sending his other set of books up in flames. The psychologist fell into the bathroom, locking the door behind him.

Guards immediately stormed into the office, Kevlar suits, riot shields and stun guns at the ready. "Get on the ground!" they howled. "Get down on your knees, put your hands behind your head, and don't move!" Seeing he had a fireball at the ready, they started firing stunner after stunner into him, but they just melted in the flames. Seeing the stun guns were no use, one shouted out "Defense Plan Beta, go!" As if second nature, the guard closest to the fire extinguisher ripped it from the wall and began spraying the white mist in Duke's direction, blocking his view. Most of the remaining guards blitzed him, pinning him to the ground under their riot shields as another one ran for the case, ripped a syringe with the blue liquid in it out and uncapped the needled, jamming the needle into Duke's neck as he tackled him. The plan worked so well that Duke didn't have a chance to respond. Within seconds, the glowing stopped and his eyes shut. He was out cold.

WASHED AWAY

The elevator leading to the cell block creaked as it came to a stop. Two guards got off the elevator carrying Duke's unconscious body, a third guard following behind. They threw Duke into his cell like a sack of dirt, his body motionless on the floor.

"What did he do this time? Kill the psychologist?" the girl in the cell across from his inquired. She was sitting on her bed, her right leg up against her chest and her right arm resting on the respective knee while her left leg sat dangling off the edge. She looked up into the eyes of the guards, her sapphire hair glistening with grease and sweat that had accumulated since her last shower.

"He just lost his temper," stated one of the guards. "There's nothing you need to know beyond that, Eleanor."

"It's 'Lia!'" she rebuked, leaning forward. "Two years and you still can't get it right," she whispered under her breath. "Amazing how prison security can be so thick."

"Whatever," he said, opening the door and tossing a set of chains at her. "Put these on."

"Hey, buddy," shouted the black man kitty-corner from Lia, "no one else down here is going to be causing any trouble to the staff besides

Duke, and from the drool around his mouth, you have him pretty well under control."

"Virgil," spat one of the other guards, "just shut up. You know why we require you to wear these chains when we take any of you out of the cellblock." Once Virgil had turned around and sat back against the wall, the guard turned back to Lia. "Palms up, hands out, and start walking." He waved his stunner at the elevator.

As the elevator doors closed, Lia looked at the one which had waved for her to get on and said, "I'm not like Duke, you know. I don't need to be restrained like this, and you had no right telling Virgil to be quiet. He has freedom of speech, just as all you do."

One of the guards turned to her, a look of annoyance easily read from his eyes. "Just shut your face." He turned back around, facing away from her.

"No," she quickly retorted. "I'll complain all I want, and you can't stop me because it's not obstructing your personal liberties."

The guards just looked back at her, but nothing else was said until they got to a conference room across the hall from Dr. Leon's office. "Welcome, Lia," he said, looking up from across the 3'x9' steel table. "Please, take a seat." He gestured towards the metal chair across from him.

"Thank you, sir," she said, walking over to the table and sitting down, her elbows resting on the table. "I hope Duke didn't hurt you too badly."

"Oh, no," Leon affirmed as he clicked his pen and flipped to a new sheet of paper. "He didn't hurt anyone, luckily. He lost his temper, so we had to give him a mild sedative."

"Like usual," Lia smirked.

Leon couldn't help but snicker at her comment. "An unfortunate circumstance, but part of who he is nonetheless." Dr. Leon pushed a button on the phone next to him and said, "Sergeant, we're ready whenever you're ready."

"I'll be there in a minute," came a voice over the speaker. It however wasn't even a minute until the door opened and Sergeant Russell came in. "Well, good to see you again," he said to Leon, "and you too, Lia," he said as he looked up at her, though she didn't make eye contact. "The President wants updated files. So, there's just a few questions to answer."

"Do you want me to just list off all the information for you then, or would you like to ask every question?"

Russell clicked his pen and opened her file. "If you know all the information we need, go ahead and start."

"Very well then," she said, scratching her forehead. "My name is Eleanor Cordelia Neptuosa, but I go by 'Lia.' I was born January 19th, 2001, which makes me seventeen. I'm 5'4" and 110 pounds with sapphire hair and blue eyes. Does that answer all your questions?"

He wrote for a couple seconds more before saying, "We just need to know about allergies or any other medical conditions."

"I have no known allergies, and no known medical conditions besides my powers."

"Finally, we need an updated background story out of you."

She frowned and scoffed at him. "Again?" Before he could respond, she started her story. "I was born and raised in a small town in Indiana, the name of which escapes me right now. My mother had me when she was fourteen and a freshman in high school. She had been 'dating' a young boy for three or four years up to that point, and he had just turned 21. Her parents knew nothing of him until she was pregnant with me. He decided that it was time to take the relationship to the next step, even though she said 'no' more than once. Being bigger and stronger, it wasn't hard for him to have his way with her. Shortly after, her parents found out, and my grandfather, in a blind rage, hunted him down and took a metal bat to him. He's currently serving a life sentence in a state prison in Indiana.

"That left my grandmother to not only finish raising her daughter, whom she reprimanded for not resisting, but to raise a granddaughter as well. My mother and grandmother were scorned by the church they attended. Being fundamentalists, my mother was accused of being 'sexually deviant' and was openly called a 'whore' by fellow congregants and Reverend Screech. My grandmother was accused of poor parenting and verbally backstabbed by her friends. Suffice it to say, I was never baptized because I was already 'damned.'

"As for home life, I never remember my mother taking care of me when I was sad, mad, hungry, sick, anything. I was the child that shouldn't be, and my mother couldn't stand the sight of me, I'm sure. She even denied I was her daughter after a while. My mother disowned me and my grandmother put me up for adoption when I was nine. I was tossed around the foster care system. The depression really got to me, and it eventually peaked with the flash flood that decimated all of Fort Wayne. Somehow they were able to connect the dots. I was soon taken in and found guilty of over 300,000 deaths and over $5B in property damage. I was locked up in a maximum security prison, I don't remember where. Once this facility was built, I was placed here so I was as far away from society as possible."

Russell finished writing the sentences and clicked his pen. "Okay," he said, looking up at them. "I will go type this all up and send it in." He walked out of the room.

"In that case," Leon commented, "we can begin our session."

"If we must," Lia sighed.

"Why do you not want to have a session with me?"

"Because nothing is different from the last time. So, what's the point?" She got up to stare at her reflection in the two-way mirror, her arms crossed.

"Well, I still need to turn in reports on the mental status of the Four, which includes you, my child. So, as much as I'd like to send you back to your cell and not have you feel like I'm wasting your time or have you feel I'm wasting my own time, we all have our orders here." He gave her a half-smile before asking, "So how have you been feeling?"

"I've been feeling like I'd like to get out of this place." She looked down and ran her fingers through her greasy hair.

"I'm sure you do," murmured Leon, the half-smile fading. "However, with how much death and destruction you and the other three have already caused and how much of a danger society views you four as being until you all learn to control your respective powers, it is in the best interests of all nations to have you four locked up and away from any country."

"I understand that, but I still find it pathetic."

"If I were in your shoes, I'm sure I'd feel the same way."

"You however never have been in my shoes. So, please, never pretend to know what it's like to live my life."

"How right you are. Let's just continue on, then. How has your appetite been?"

"I eat what I'm given. So, healthy I guess."

"Very good. What about your relations with the others?"

"I've tried having conversations with Aria with occasional success, but she just isn't a great conversation holder. What conversations we do have don't last long or go very in-depth. Virgil and I have tried having conversations as well, but it inevitably always leads to him thinking I'm just like every other White person, which ends the conversation fairly quickly. As for Duke, he and I argue like none other, as I'm sure he's already told you." She turned back to face him. "Can I go back to my cell now?"

"I have no other questions to ask, so, why not?" He waved the guards over to take her back. One of the guards put a hand on her shoulder and guided her out of the room. Once the door had closed behind them, he wrote down in his notes, *Duke and Lia are going to make a great couple.*

A ROCKY PAST

The walk back from Dr. Leon's office was as silent as the walk there, if not quieter. Then again, there wasn't much to say, since Lia wouldn't disclose any information on her personal life to guards who more or less couldn't care less anyway. The silence was finally broken by the sound of the elevator leading to the cells.

"In you go," one of the guards said, opening her cell door and unlocking her restraints.

"As if I could go anywhere else," Lia replied. She laid down on her bed, staring up the vast shaft overhead.

As her cell door closed, one of the other guards was already opening the door to Virgil's cell. "Get up," he ordered, throwing the restraints to him, "and put those one."

Virgil looked up, glaring at the guards. "And if I don't, what are you all going to do to me?"

"Just put them on, Virgil," Lia asserted. "They're just taking you to Dr. Leon's office."

"As if that makes any difference," he retorted. "Some rich White dude who takes pride in watching his hand write wrong guesses as to what's wrong with me; as if that's the person I want to see."

"Just shut up and put them on," came another voice, this time from the cell across from him. The girl in the cell had sat up on her bed and was now looking over at him. "You're going to be in restraints regardless. So, make it easy on yourself and put them on yourself." She laid back down and turned away from him.

"So the mute can talk," one of the guards joked. "I'd have never thunk it."

"I just thought the chemo destroyed her vocal cords," another replied. All the guards started to laugh.

"Shut up!" Lia yelled. "So what if Aria doesn't talk much, and so what if she is hairlessness with a bony structure? That doesn't give you the right to be degrading her."

"Lia, mind your own business," Virgil spat. "You wouldn't defend me, so why defend anyone else?"

"It's not always about you."

"All of you shut up!" the tall guard thundered. He looked back over at Virgil. "Put the chains on and come with us. You don't need this being any harder than it already is."

"Not like these chains can restrain me, but whatever," he said as he stood up, showing his full musculature. He strapped himself into the restraints and stepped out towards the elevator, guards surrounding him.

Once at the conference room, Dr. Leon stood up from his chair, saying, "Welcome, Virgil. Please take a seat."

Virgil just looked down at the man, shaking the guards' hands off his shoulders. "I prefer to stand," he voiced, proceeding over to the wall to Leon's right and standing with his back to it.

"Very well," Dr. Leon said, waving the guards down and walking back to his chair. Once seated, he pressed a button on the intercom, saying, "Sergeant Russell, we are ready for you here."

"Ten-four. I'm on my way. Over and out," a familiar voice responded.

"Why's he coming?" Virgil growled. "Aren't there enough skinheads around here already?"

"Virgil, they're not skinheads," Dr. Leon responded. "Just because they're bald doesn't make them skinheads, just as much as Aria's baldness doesn't make her one."

"You'd think differently if you were in my shoes, doc," he replied as he turned away from the good doctor.

The door opened suddenly, Sergeant Russell walking through and approaching Virgil. "Son," the sergeant replied, "I'm sure if everyone lived the horrors you've endured, they'd have a greater respect for you. However, your background is classified information only the various doctors, top military personnel, president, and myself are qualified to know."

"I don't need y'all's respect, and I ain't your son." Virgil pushed the sergeant away, soldiers being waved down as they responded to the aggression.

"As for why the good sergeant is here," Dr. Leon stated, "he needs you to give him your profile."

"Y'all have my profile," he snapped, breaking the chains which bound his hands together. The guards drew their tasers, but Russell waved them down again.

"The President requested it," Russell replied. "I don't have a choice in the matter. So, if you'll please just humor us, this will all be over soon."

"And why should I?" Virgil looked up at Russell, a disgusted look on his face.

Russell pulled out the box he had before and opened it, declaring, "Because I can inject you with truth serum mixed with a little tranquilizer to make you cooperative and answer the questions. It's your choice, but we will be getting the answers out of you."

"Fine, fine," Virgil agreed, holding up his hands and sitting sideways at the table. "I'd rather answer your questions than have you poison me."

"It's not poison, but good to know you'll cooperate. Shall we get started then?"

"Whatever."

"Very well. Full name?"

"Virgil Spencer Adams."

"Date of birth?"

"December 19th, 1999."

"Okay, so age is eighteen. Hair color?"

"Black."

"Eye color?"

"Brown."

"Height?"

"6'3"."

"Weight?"

"250 pounds."

"Allergies?"

"White people."

Dr. Leon choked back a laugh as Russell looked up at Virgil, shaking his head. "So none. Any other medical conditions we should be aware of?"

"No."

"Alright, and lastly, your background story."

Virgil looked up at the sergeant. "You don't need my background story. You have at least three of them on file, and they haven't changed."

"I have my orders to get it fresh, though." Russell crossed his arms and looked over at Virgil. "Please, just humor us, and we'll be out of your hair."

A long pause followed, but it was broken when Virgil asserted, "Fine, have it your way." He looked back down at the floor, and without letting Russell get ready to record, started giving his story. "My dad had a gambling problem. It started when he was in college, after he had married my mother. Needing to pay off student loans, wedding fees, car payments, baby me, and the like, he hit up the casino nearby. Running out of money, he borrowed money from two brothers who worked together as loan sharks, but he lost it all. Rather than break his fingers, they made him a deal. He, my mother, and I work as indentured servants until my dad's work had paid back all the money that was owed, and they would forgive him. Talking with my mother, she agreed. So, we lived just outside of Santa Barbara, CA on a small plantation they owned.

"Not wanting to get the authorities onto what they were up to, they provided housing and food for me and my family, and they allowed me to be enrolled in school. If I got anything below a B- on anything, though, they beat me. If the crops didn't reap a certain amount, my family was blamed, and we all were beaten. If the chores around the house weren't done, the one responsible was beaten. This went on for fourteen years.

"When I was a freshman in high school, I knew enough about U.S. history and ethics to know what the sharks were doing to my family was wrong. So, I stood up to them. My mother didn't clean all of the sheets and towels one day. So, they took her out back and were going to physically beat her. I ran out, though, tackling one of them. The other reprimanded me, slapping me for tackling his brother. His brother got up behind me and kicked me in the back of my knee, forcing me into a kneel. The first one pulled out a knife and cut my left cheek, saying that would be a sample of what they'd do if I tried it again. They pushed me aside and turned back to my mother. One of them went to slap her, and I caught his arm, twisting it behind his back, dislocating it, and my strength shattering his bone. The other pulled a knife and came at me. Being bigger than his brother and being as strong as me, we struggled. While we struggled, I felt something in me awaken. The ground beneath us began to shake violently. They lost their balance, and everyone, myself included, fell into the sinkhole that now lies where Santa Barbara once lay.

"As I was the only one to make it out alive from an earthquake they said no one should have survived, they got information from me. Figuring out where the epicenter was, and realizing it was not on a fault line, they said that I did something that caused the disaster, as there was no other explanation. They locked me up in a maximum security prison, not knowing if that would even hold me. Once this place was constructed, I was thrown in here, and here we stand."

Russell continued writing for a few seconds, then clicked his pen. "I'll type this up and send it in. Thanks for your cooperation." He walked away, not looking back to see Virgil give him the finger.

"Now we can begin our session," Dr. Leon said, clicking his own pen. "How have you been feeling?"

"Since I'm the only Black person here, alone, abandoned by society."

"You however are not alone or abandoned. You have the other three, who are guilty of crimes much like your own, and who have backgrounds as horrifying as yours. So, you are not as alone as you think you are, and you are not abandoned by society. I am here for you as a representative of the rest of society, bringing with me all the fears and intrigue society has for the Four."

"Not that that's in any way reassuring, but okay. Next question."

"Very well. How has your appetite been?"

"I've eaten what I've been given."

"So healthy. How have your conversations with the other three been?"

"They're White, like the men who beat my parents and me. Why should I show them any light of day, especially after what I've been through?"

"Not all White people are bad. Am I a bad person?"

"You're a professional doing your job. What you're like outside your work could be completely different than how you're being right now. So, I can't answer that question."

Leon continued to scribble on his notepad. "Assume I am like this outside the job spectrum as well. Am I a bad person?"

"Well, no, but one person out of billions isn't going to represent what all of society is like."

"And you just got at what I've been driving towards for two years," Leon remarked, smiling. He took his glasses off and set his notepad aside. "I know it is hard for you to accept after what you have endured. Hell, some people still aren't over their segregating mindsets. However, those persons are not a representation of all of the human race. They are individuals who represent themselves. Are you exactly like Duke or myself?"

"No."

"Exactly. You are an individual. You are unique, representing not all of society, but yourself and yourself alone. It may take time to accept that, but this is what I hope to help you learn."

"Whatever. Can I go back to my cell now?" Virgil turned away from the psychologist.

"Well, I have no more questions for you. So, if you have no questions for me, I don't see why not." He pressed a button, signaling a few of the guards standing outside to come take him back.

IV

ROGUE GUST

The sound of the elevator descending into the cell block startled Lia, who had not realized she had fallen asleep. She looked over in time to see Virgil guided off the elevator, unshackled, and locked back in his cell. "Looks like it's your turn," she commented to Aria.

Aria didn't say anything. She just stared at the guards turning and unlocking her door from a corner of her cell.

"Here you go, baldy," one of the guards spat, tossing the chains across the cell. They hit the ground and slid for a few feet, stopping just a couple inches from where Aria sat. She silently got them on and walked onto the elevator.

Not a word was spoken until they got to the conference room. "Here's the last one," the tallest guard stated, pushing Aria through the door and closing it behind him.

"Well, it's good to see you again, Aria," Dr. Leon said, smiling over at her from across the table. "Please, have a seat." He motioned towards the other chair.

Aria nodded to him and took a seat, staring at the table. Though she had been in here before, she only ever really looked at the floor or the table.

"Sergeant Russell will be in to create an updated report in just a second," Leon told her, "and then we can begin our session." Aria just nodded in response to him.

A few moments passed before the door opened again, Russell walking through the door with a clipboard in his hand and a pen behind his ear. "Good to see you again," he remarked, looking back and forth between Dr. Leon and Aria. Both nodded in response, but Leon was the only one to look at him. "Shall we get started then?"

"Sure," Aria murmured, maintaining focus on the table.

"Very well, then." Russell clicked his pen and placed it against the paper. "What is your full name?"

"Aria Rose Harmos."

"How about your date of birth?"

"April 23rd, 2001."

"So you're seventeen years old. Your hair color?"

"I'm naturally bald."

"Eye color?"

"Gray."

"Height?"

"5'1"."

"Weight?"

"100 pounds."

"Allergies?"

"None."

"Any other known medical conditions?"

"No."

"Okay," Russell continued as he turned the page, "all I need now is your background story."

"Where do you want me to start?"

Astounded she hadn't put up an argument as the other three had, he took a double take, quickly regaining his composure. "As far back as you can remember."

"I was born into a family of politicians. My mother was a circuit court judge while my father was a state senator in Maine. As a result, my family was very rich. I was the youngest of two boys and two girls. By the time I was three, my father was running for the governorship.

However, he wouldn't have pictures taken, at least not while I was around, because he felt my unusual baldness would somehow tarnish his image and ruin his chances of getting elected. So, I was kept home for most of his first campaign. They homeschooled me instead of sending me to the private school my brothers and sister were attending at the time. At the same time though, they took me to the best dermatologists and hair care specialists in the nation. The doctors didn't find anything wrong with me, not like there was anything wrong, and the hair care specialists' treatments did nothing. They spent an unreasonable amount of money trying to make me into something I wasn't. They gave up on that endeavor by the time I was eight or nine. So, they bought me a wig to wear whenever I went out in public. The public loved getting to meet me finally, and people even commented I helped my father get his second term as governor. However, I was an outcast in my own home. No one ever told me they loved me for who I really was. The public may have loved me, yes, but for being someone I wasn't. The public didn't even know about my 'condition' until I pretty much destroyed the state capital."

"And why did you do that?" Russell inquired, looking up from his note taking.

"My father's second term as governor was coming to a close. I was thirteen at the time. He was giving a public speech on a new bill which had recently passed that would increase taxes but would also give schools statewide more money per student. He ended it saying, 'I have high hopes for all my children as well as your children in the coming years, for they are our future.' Since he basically never looked at me or showed me any affection, I burst out with, 'Really, father? You have hope even for me?' I then tore off my wig and threw it on the ground, continuing with, 'You homeschool me because I have no hair and because it would hurt your image. So, since when have you ever given a damn about my future or my interests, even in how I'm taught?' He kindly told me to sit down and put my wig back on, all the while smiling for the camera. My siblings tried to restrain me, and my mother covered my mouth. I threw them all off of me. I continued to rant in front of a live audience and twenty-some cameras, completely blowing a gasket on my father. I don't remember what all I said, but I do remember my final words to him were, 'I hate you! Just die already!' It was then the winds started picking up to hurricane speeds. People were blown off their feet, buildings collapsed, and everyone except for me was killed. I was caught a few days later thanks to all the videos being shot at the speech. I was charged with the assassination of the governor, 39 senators and representatives, and other visiting politicians, and with the murder of about a hundred other people, including my mother and siblings. So, I was put in a maximum security prison for about a year. Then this place was built, and I've been here since."

"Might I ask something else, off the record?" Russell inquired, clicking his pen and placing it back behind his ear. "Why didn't you complain like the other three?"

"I'd be made to answer if I didn't do it on my own. So, saving time and truth serum."

Russell paused at her answer, not sure whether to be thankful for her honesty or to pity her for her overly-easy submission. "Fair enough," he breathed, flipping the pages back over and walking towards the door. "I guess I'll send this on then," he announced as he opened the door and walked out again.

"Well," Leon began, "shall we begin our session?" He placed his glasses back on.

"Sure," Aria replied. Her eyes lifted to meet Leon's eyes for the first time in months.

"Okay, how have you been feeling lately?"

"Neutral emotionally, though with spurts of happiness and sadness."

"How so with the spurts?"

"My sister's twenty-first birthday would have been last week. So, I miss her, but at the same time, I'm happy she's dead, because she was just as rude to me as my father. So, it fluctuates as my thoughts wander and progress."

"I see, very interesting." Leon scribbled a few more notes down before asking her, "How about your appetite?"

"I've eaten what I've been given."

"So, as healthy as can be assumed. How have your communications with the other three been?"

"I don't talk much, still."

"Is there a reason why?"

"I was taught to never talk unless spoken to, and even then to speak pre-written lines. I don't know if I'll ever get used to having free speech, even if I did have that outburst all those years ago."

"A valid point; what we learn and are trained to do or believe as children does set a foundation for how we live the rest of our lives. However, certain aspects can be untrained, like your unfamiliarity and even discomfort with free speech. That is what I've tried to accomplish with you. You are a knowledgeable young woman, and what you have to say can be of benefit to humanity as a whole, as is true with any person. So, try talking with them more, see where your conversations lead you. You'll become more comfortable with it as time goes on, I promise."

Aria stared at him for a few seconds, then finally replied, "I'll try." She then got up and walked towards the door. "I assume this session is over."

"Unless you have any questions for me, yes."

"I have none."

"Then it is over." He pressed a button next to him, and the guards from before came in to escort her back to her cell.

V

THE FOUR AS ONE

The elevator finally reached the cell block. As Aria got off, she noticed Lia and Virgil lying awake on their beds, Duke still knocked out on the floor of his cell. The guards unlocked her shackles and pushed her inside her cell, closing and locking the door behind her. As she sat down on her bed, her chin resting on her knees and her arms wrapped around her legs, the doors to the elevator closed and ascended to the top of the shaft.

Nothing was said until Duke began moving again. Slowly but surely, he picked himself up and hobbled over to his bed, still slightly under the effects of the tranquilizer. "How long was I out?" he asked, sitting down, head in his hands.

"A few hours, give or take," Lia responded, sitting up and looking over at him. "Good of you to finally join us."

"Hey, shut up!" He let his hands drop and looked over at her. "I'd like to see you join us all after a session with that man."

"See, that's the irony," she remarked, "because you're the only one ever to be brought back with a syringe hole in their neck. Everyone else can control themselves, both their powers and their tempers."

"Yeah, flooding a whole city and killing hundreds of thousands, that shows real control," Duke scoffed.

"That was years ago and you know it. You, on the other hand, burned half of Dr. Leon's records and resources for no good reason, and that was just earlier today."

Duke, finally gaining full control of himself again, stood up and walked over to the wall across from Lia. "He compared me to my father."

"Like I said, you did it for no good reason."

"Hey, if you had the kind of father I had-"

"The kind of father you had?" she repeated, standing up and walking towards him. "My father was killed by my grandfather, so I grew up without any kind of father figure. I didn't have much of a mother figure either. At least your father acknowledged your existence."

"I'd have rather he hadn't! My life wouldn't be so screwed up if it weren't for him!"

"Shut up, you two!" Virgil yelled, standing up and staring at them both. "At least you two had freedom growing up! My family and I were forced to work without pay!"

"And as far as you know, you may very well be in the same place as you are now, even if you had freedom," Lia stated. "With the powers you have, who wouldn't lock you, or any of us for that matter, up far away from the rest of civilization?"

"I would have greater control though because of the nurturing I would have received," Virgil replied.

"Not true," Aria cried, placing her feet on the ground. "My family were in the eyes of the media constantly, and were loved by everyone they ever met. Yet, look at where I am now. You have no idea how you would have been nurtured if your parents hadn't been more-or-less enslaved."

"Like you would know, baldy!"

"Hey, leave her alone!" Lia screeched.

"I don't need you standing up for me," Aria spat.

"As if you would stand up for yourself," Duke replied. "Do you even know how to stand up for yourself?"

"I killed hundreds of people and destroyed a state capital all because I stood up for myself. So, I'd say, 'yes.'"

"More like PMS, if you ask me." Duke began to snicker.

"Unfortunately, no one did ask you.'"

"Like you would know what PMS does to a person anyway," Lia replied. "Not that you have the parts to be a man either."

"Oh, you just got shut down!" Virgil started laughing, Aria following suit soon after.

"You saying I'm not well-equipped? Well, check out this equipment." Duke dropped his pants to his ankles. "I don't have the right parts you say? What are these then?" He pulled his pants back up.

The other three just looked at him in disbelief, eyes wide and mouths ajar. Lia finally broke the silence, saying, "I can't believe you just did that!"

Duke just stood there, cracking up after a few moment, saying, "I can't either!" He fell to the ground laughing. The other three started cracking up soon after. Within moments, all four were on the floor crying because they were laughing so hard, none of them anticipating their conversation would have gone that route.

The laughter went on for over half an hour, the Four finally settling down. Lia was the first to talk again, saying, "Even if we don't get along all the time, these moments of enjoyment are well-worth it."

"Agreed," the other three voiced.

The sound of the elevator descending caught all of their attention. "Lunch time," Aria added. They all took a seat on their beds and waited for their meals to be slid through a slot on their doors.

In the surveillance room sat twenty screens, ten of which were focused on the cell block, the other ten disbursed throughout the complex.

Dr. Leon and Sergeant Russell sat behind the control panel, watching the Four intently. "As you can see," Leon stated, "even amongst the most bleak of settings, there is always hope for change, and drastic changes at that."

"Yeah, right," Russell remarked. "I'll be convinced when I see Duke cuddling up with a puppy he names after his father."

"Why do you hate them so?" Leon looked over at the man, disbelieving the sarcasm in Russell's tone of voice.

"They are disgraces to the human race! They're freaks! They have killed more people than are in the state of Rhode Island, and if we let them out, we'll have our first mass genocide of the century. They cannot be let free, ever."

"They can be let free, and they will be eventually, whether you like it or not."

"And when they are, I'll be the one to take the kill shot on all four of them." He pretended to be aiming a sniper rifle at each of their heads and made the motion of pulling the trigger, making a sound of gun fire as he did.

"Sometimes I wonder whether or not we should be locking you up with them." Leon began walking towards the door.

"And sometimes I wonder whether or not you're the one who needs counseling."

Leon stopped and turned around. "At least counseling would have an effect on me. You're just a hopeless case, lost to the world." Leon closed the door behind him.

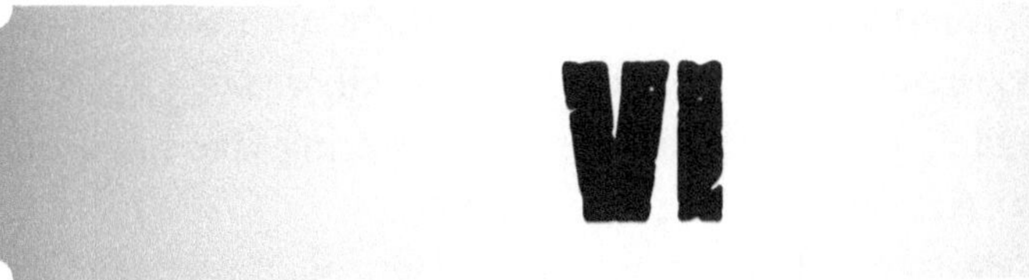

REVELATION BY LIGHT

The Four had fallen asleep shortly after the Sun went down, a placid silence spreading across the island. Even the water that so recently crashed on the shorelines fell still as the night was called forth. In the middle of this peace descended from the heavens a ball of light. It slowly passed through the glass covering over the shaft, through the steel panels, and down into the cell block. As it touched down, the ball of light grew and formed itself into the human form of Artaxerxes. His long, flowing white hair fell over His white robes, His youthful face and skin illuminating the darkness, and His eyes shone with the light of a newborn star.

He looked around the circular room, and in so doing willed all time to stop outside of the cell block. He began walking around. *Tonight marks a new beginning for these four*, He thought to Himself. "Awaken," He proclaimed, shattering the silence. "Wake up, O Chosen Ones, and listen to my words."

The Four all began moving, looking over at where Artaxerxes stood and quickly covering their eyes from the light resonating from Him. "What the Hell?" Duke spat. "Am I still dreaming?" He pinched himself hard, jolting in reaction, the mysterious man still present. "Apparently not." He turned to see the other three shielding their eyes from the light, groaning at having been abruptly awoken as well.

"No, my children," He declared to them, looking around to meet each of their eyes, reducing His glow so they might not need to shield their eyes, "you are not dreaming. I am as real as all of you."

"Who the Hell are you?" Lia pressed, lowering her hand and walking towards Artaxerxes.

"Really," Virgil and Aria agreed, sitting up on their beds and lowering their hands as well.

"And we're not your children," Duke added, lowering his hands. "I've already had one father in my life. That's more than enough for my lifetime."

"You are my children, though," Artaxerxes affirmed. "I am Artaxerxes: the Alpha and the Omega, the Creator of all things. Therefore, you are my children."

"Uh huh," Duke retorted, "sure you are."

He turned and looked deep into Duke's eyes. "You always were resistant to those in power, Duke." A smile cracked across His face. "Soon enough, you will believe and follow, just as many before you have." He turned back to all of them. "Duke, Aria, Virgil and Lia, blessed are you among mortals, for you have been gifted with great power over the elements, and are fated for great things."

"How do you know our names, creeper?" Aria asked.

"I know your names because, as I said, I am the Beginning and the End, King of kings and Lord of lords. I have watched all of you from on high, seeing you grow and tap into your powers for eighteen years now, and I must say I am well-pleased." The smile that was on His face then disappeared, a look of concern quickly replacing the joy that once was there. "However, there is still more to do, more for you four to know, more for you all to accomplish."

"Okay, time out, buddy," Duke said, making a "T" with his hands. "You keep claiming to be God, but, if God exists, then we wouldn't be here. I wouldn't have been abused by my father, nor would he have turned to alcohol or my mother died giving birth to me. Lia's mother and grandmother wouldn't have rejected her, nor would a congregation of people claiming to be devoted followers of you have done the same.

Aria's parents wouldn't have been so self-centered and ignorant of her needs. As for Virgil, his father wouldn't have been a gambling addict, and the more-or-less slave owners would have been caught long ago. Not to mention all the towns that were destroyed and all the people that died wouldn't be decimated or deceased. If you are God and you are so great, tell me then why all this has happened. How could so great a being as 'God' let this happen?"

The other three looked at each other, amazed at the logic behind what the hothead had said, shaking their heads in agreement and voicing a "yeah" along with it, frowning at the great white man.

Artaxerxes smiled. *Already, the leader arises from a slumber, bringing them from four to one.* "A valid question," He replied. "I shall answer your question with one of my own. If I were to let you all out into the world, powers fully under control, would you all not seek out those doing injustice and right the wrongs of this world? Would you all not fight for what is right, stand for those who cannot stand and speak for those who are without voice?"

Duke lifted his finger to pose an argument, but just as he was about to make a sound, he paused. Whether or not this man was who he said he was, he had a valid point. Duke's finger curled back and his hand lowered as his eyes hit the floor, realizing this stranger was right.

Artaxerxes' smile faded and He turned back to all four of them. "I allowed what happened to you all to happen that you all might be led to a single mindset, a belief, if you will, that this world is filled with injustice, and that such injustice must be brought to its knee and that reparations might be paid."

"You still haven't told us why you're here, though," Virgil interjected. "Are you here to train us? To set us free?"

He turned to look Virgil right in the eyes, His palms up and to the side slightly. "Like I said, I have been watching you all for eighteen years, and I am the one who created the four elemental spirits which reside within each of you. As has been foretold, I come to help you along on the development of your powers. You will gain an understanding of why later, once you all have left this place. For now, though, I give you back knowledge left dormant until now and a slight increase in strength. So, clear your minds, that such gifts might be given." The Four, slightly groggy and not sure whether what He said bore any truth, did as He commanded, and began to levitate in their cells. They felt their power levels and their physical strength grow second by second. They felt their brains pulsating as they regained memories of how to fly and how they could use their powers and better control them, eventually coming to a full understanding of the magnitude of their powers.

When it was all over, they were returned to their beds, each of them now asleep again. Artaxerxes unfroze time and ascended back into the heavens, a new age now begun.

VII

NOT A DREAM

As the sunlight shone once more, it sought out all shadows, banishing them back into the oblivion from which they came crawling hours before. It soon enough spread to the shores of the facility and down the shaft, piercing through the ceiling.

The Four began groaning as the light, along with the sound of the main elevator descending from the world above, woke them. They covered their heads with their pillows and sheets to avoid fully waking up, but it was of no use.

Duke eventually sat up and wiped his eyes. "What a weird night," he recounted. He looked up the shaft and saw a few guards and the facility's maid entering the elevator above. "Looks like it's shower day."

Lia looked up in the direction of the elevator, and sighed. "At least we can get a warm shower as a trade off for sleep, for what it's worth anyway." She and the other two arose from their beds, waiting for the guards and the maid to arrive.

When they finally arrived, they were each handed a towel, shackled together in a line, and surrounded by guards who then escorted them to the shower room at the top of the elevator. Once there, they were unshackled and shoved inside the glass chamber. They each entered a shower cell along the back wall, stripped out of their uniform, hung it up with their towel, and turned the water on.

As Lia cleaned herself, she saw her reflection in the fogged glass, noticing something was a bit off. She stopped scrubbing herself and began turning in different directions. *Something's not right,* she thought, running her hands down her body. *What could it be, though?* Suddenly, she realized she wasn't touching the floor and gasped. "Um, guys," she called out, "are any of you touching the floor?"

The other three stopped scrubbing themselves as well, wondering if they heard her right. "Did you just ask if we are touching the floor?" Virgil asked.

"Answer my question," she spat, fear present in her voice. "Are you or are you not touching the floor?"

"What kind of a question is that?" Duke mocked. "Of course we're . . . Holy shit! She's right! Aria, Virgil, look at your feet!" He could hear gasps coming from their shower cells as they realized they too were levitating. No one responded. They just kept scrubbing themselves down, silent and wide-eyed the rest of the time. By the time the steam had cleared, though, they all had touched back down, not knowing how or when they even began to levitate.

Once they got back to their cells, they found a tray with oatmeal and a glass of water as well as fresh uniforms in each of their cells. They were unshackled, locked back in their cells, and left to their meal. The Four ate in unusual silence, no one knowing quite what to say.

Virgil was the one to finally break the silence, saying, "So, that levitation thing, I was given knowledge of how to do it in a dream last night, but I thought it was just that, a dream, even if it did seem oddly real." Duke and Aria began to audibly choke on their oatmeal at the mention of a strange dream.

Lia, hearing his words, looked at him in shock, the surprise causing her to break the glass she held with seemingly little effort. *I've never been able to do that before,* she thought. She dropped the shards to the ground in surprise, but there was no blood, cuts, or slivers. Her hand was uninjured; yet another surprise. The other three looked in amazement. "Artaxerxes?" she asked, unable to say anything else.

"Artaxerxes," the other three echoed, realizing what they initially thought was a dream was in fact very real.

"If he gave us this knowledge though, that would mean we're in control of it." She set her stuff down on her bed, and, willing herself to levitate, rose into the air with no effort at all. "Whoa! I wonder if this means we can really fly." She willed herself to move, and she did. She rose and descended, moved every which way, finally sitting back down on her bed. *We can fly!* A smile went right across her face.

"So we can fly," Virgil remarked, killing the moment. "My question is what else we can do."

"Let's leave that for later," Aria commented. "Artaxerxes mentioned He wants us out of here for some reason or another. The problem is how it's going to happen. There are guards at every door in the facility. Breaking a window or a door would set off an alarm."

"Well," Virgil articulated, "we either have to break through the hordes of guards or break a hole in the floor and go through massive amounts of dirt and such in the hopes of ending up on the other side of the walls. Even then, we have what seems like an endless body of water on all sides with the only way out being the ferry which brings guards and other workers over. We could fly, but who knows where and when we'd hit land."

"Well, think about it, though," Lia interjected. "If we head in any direction, we're bound to hit land. If we fly in the direction the ferry travels, that's the direction of the U.S."

"That still doesn't answer how we get out," Duke pointed out. "We either need to take a direct route through the guards, or we take the alternative route and push our way through tons of dirt, rock, and clay. That being our alternative, I vote we choose Curtain #1."

"Meaning you'd fight your way through the most well-trained and well-armed guards on Earth," Lia asserted. "You forget, we're in the prison of all prisons right now. No one gets in or out without written consent of the Secretary of Defense. Besides, we're the four most-dangerous kids on the face of the Earth. Foreign powers *paid* to build this facility. We aren't going to be able to just walk around the streets when we do get out. We need connections, and unfortunately, I don't have any connections like that. Do any of you?"

"We don't need connections," Duke stated, frowning at Lia. "All we need is a place to hide out. Of our four hometowns, mine is both the closest and the least likely to have anyone living there. So, we fly there and we hide out there, at least until we can come up with somewhere better."

A brief silence fell among them. "That's as good of an idea as any," Aria soon voiced. "I say we go for it."

"How do we get out, then?" Virgil asked, returning them to the immediate issue.

"We take down all those guards," Duke replied.

Aria looked unsurprised, but worried. "You actually mean to take this 'direct approach' and storm through the doors and take down everyone you can?"

"In short, yes. It will take all four of us to do it, though. I know we're not usually cooperative with each other, but for now, we need each other if we mean to get out of this Hell hole alive the way Artaxerxes wants us. So, if you're in on a little revenge along with a little escape, say 'I.'"

"I," Virgil replied immediately, cracking his knuckles and smiling.

"I," Lia agreed. "I want out of here, and I want to know more about why we were chosen by Artaxerxes."

"I," Aria said after a few seconds of consideration. "Let's do it."

"Well, it looks like we're all in," Duke declared. "First, we need to break down our cell doors. Does that sound good?"

"Hold on a second," Lia inserted, scratching her chin with a smile on her face. "I just thought of something. Why don't we just go straight up? This shaft goes directly to the surface, and the glass is no thicker above us than in front of us. Plus, if we are as strong as Artaxerxes seems to have made us, the steel ceiling doesn't stand a chance. It's faster and avoids conflict."

"Fair enough," Duke sighed after a brief moment of thought, agreeing with Lia but disappointed at being denied his "revenge." "Let us assume for a hot second, though, that we can't go all the way up *because* the steel is in fact thicker or we aren't as strong as Artaxerxes seems to have made us. That means we'd have to find a different route and could get separated or even lost in this place. So, where should we meet up at should we get separated?"

A silence fell among them as they each tried to think of a safe place. "How about the docks?" Aria suggested.

"It's as good a place as any," Duke agreed. "So, once we get out of here, should we get separated, go whatever way you can, and meet up by the pier in no more than an hour. Okay?"

"Sounds good to me," Lia, Aria and Virgil agreed.

"Does anyone else find it odd that we haven't been stormed with guards while we've been talking?" Lia asked.

"Where would they take us?" Duke asked. "We're in our cells now, and there isn't any 'solitary confinement,' at least none that we've seen or heard about in the two to three years of being here."

"No, she's right," Virgil defended. "No one's come down the elevator this whole time."

Aria started gagging, pulling a piece of paper out of her mouth, spilling some oatmeal back into her bowl. She opened it up, reading, "Artaxerxes spoke. Told 2 cut wires. Surveillance off."

"That would explain it," Virgil said. "Does the note say anything else?"

"Yeah, 'Power outage @ 10a.'" Just as she finished saying that, the lights went off and the doors unlocked. She pushed on her door and it flew open with the greatest of ease. The other three followed suit.

"How do we get up the elevator though if there's no power?" Lia asked.

"We break through the ceilings," Duke replied, "as was originally planned. If we have all this extra strength and control, let's use it." He looked around and got no disagreements. "Okay everyone, on the count of three. One . . . two . . . three . . ." The Four burst from the floor and through the glass ceiling, quickly ascending and breaking the other ceilings as well. As they broke out, Duke threw a giant fireball back into the shaft below and watched it go off like the Fourth of July, the other three caught in the fire, but flying out seconds later.

The Four were finally out.

FREE AT LAST

The flames and smoke rose high into the air, creating a thick, black cloud over the island and raining ash down onto the ground. The heat could be felt all the way down at the pier, the embers and the smoke visible for miles.

Duke stared at his inferno, chills racing down his spine out of satisfaction. *I think these powers are going to work just fine,* he thought to himself. *I wonder where the other three are.* He continued staring at the flames.

Soon after, he noticed the other three on their way to the pier.

"It took you three long enough," Duke remarked once they had landed.

"Duke, shut up!" Lia retorted, giving Duke an upper cut to the chin and sending him off his feet. "You could have killed us, you bastard!"

"And your point is?" he asked, rubbing his chin. He stood back up, glaring at Lia.

"What do you mean?" Aria spat. "You need us, just like we need you, like it or not."

"We're reincarnations of deities," he shouted, looking away from Lia. "Do you think a few flames will hurt us?"

"When they come from one of us, yes, they can," Virgil interjected. "Can you really be so thick-headed?"

"Virgil, shut your face!" Duke hollered.

"*Everyone* shut your faces!" Aria screamed. "Look, there's something moving in the fire!"

Everyone looked over, and she was right. Out of the fire stumbled Sergeant Russell, burnt all over, falling to the ground about twenty feet from the Four. "You four won't get away with this," he gasped, looking up at them, a pistol in his hand. "The U.S. Armed Forces know you've escaped, as does the President. They are ready to take you down on sight, and even if they fail, the country is under Terrorist Level Red and will be until you are all apprehended."

The Four looked at each other, Lia breaking the silence. "Is that supposed to scare us or something?"

"Yes," he replied in a raspy voice. "Be very afraid." Russell pulled the pistol and fired on Duke. The bullet hit him square in the chest, but the bullet dropped to the ground, not a mark on him. Russell dropped the gun, jaw dropped and shaking. "God help us all," he prayed, frozen on the ground.

"My turn," Duke stated, kicking him in the face as hard as he could. Russell rocketed off the ground, his face dented inward, and landed in the water beyond the horizon. "Oh ho ho ho ho . . . I could get used to this," Duke said with a smirk across his face.

"If you're done being a monster," Aria interjected, a look of disgust on her face, "we should get out of here, before the Armed Forces arrive." The Four took to the air, heading in the direction they remembered the ferry bringing them.

At about the half-way point, battleships and emerging submarines came into sight, followed closely by fighter jets. Within seconds, all began to fire on the Four, bullets coming at them from all directions.

"They're everywhere!" Duke cried.

"Your point being?" Lia asked as a wave of her creation tipped one ship into another, sinking both in one massive explosion.

"You're not scared, are you Duke?" Aria taunted, sending a fighter jet spiraling towards the ocean below with a strong gust of wind.

"Of course I'm not scared," he retaliated. "Why would I be?"

"You just sounded scared to us," Lia replied.

"Well, I'm not," he shouted. "Besides, it looks like you and Aria have things under control here. So, you focus on the battleships, and Aria," he shouted behind him, "you take care of the fighter jets."

"Why on our lonesome?" Aria hollered. "That's awfully unfair the women have to do all the work here."

"Aria, now's not the time to argue," he thundered back, avoiding cannon fire all the while. "Virgil and I will head forward to take on any other approaching forces. Just head west after you're done, and don't wait for the other."

"Fine," Lia shouted. "Just don't mess this up for us."

"Hey, think about who you're talking about," he asserted slyly.

"*Just go!*" Aria thundered, ramming a fighter jet and taking out its wing.

Lia hadn't been paying attention to this last part of the conversation, having flown towards the group of battleships after her reluctant agreement to the plan. The submarines had submerged for the time being. Flying between two of the battleships, they both fired in hopes of hitting her, but she quickly evaded, the shells hitting the other ship instead. That was two more ships down, and seemed like five or six more to go, plus the subs.

Aria was fairing pretty well herself. She had caught one jet and threw it into another, causing an explosion whose shockwave set the other jets off balance. While they fought to regain control, she spun them all by either pushing upwards or downwards on a wing, a couple of the pilots ejecting immediately. Half of the jets were now disposed.

Lia continued to evade shots, even causing one cannon to shoot down a fighter jet, much to her pleasure. She got tired of the running ploy, though, deciding play time was over. So, she created a whirlpool, pulling the ships in to the center and eventually pulling the subs in as well. Seeing a way of ending this battle now, she yelled up to Aria, "Send the jets down here! We can sink them all in one big blow!"

Aria couldn't make out what Lia had just said, but saw the whirlpool and had figured out what was intended by it. So, she created a jet stream which hit all the jets and forced them into the whirlpool, the impact between jets, battleships, and subs causing an explosion out of the water.

The whirlpool closed in, and all soldiers thus far had been sunk. Aria joined up with Lia, and they continued on their way.

When they met up with Duke and Virgil, both were engaged in battle with ground troops. Vehicles were being blown sky high, the Earth underneath the soldiers shaking and splitting in two. Hundreds of soldiers lay fried on the ground, vehicles were ablaze, and still others had been impaled by stalagmites. The sound of gunfire had been audible for a couple miles in all directions.

Duke was the one to spot the girls first. He shouted to them, "Just keep going! We'll hold them off and follow up the rear!"

Lia and Aria gave the thumbs up. Duke and Virgil gave one last blow to the forces and came up behind them.

The Four were in the clear for the time being.

DARKNESS REVEALED

The expansiveness of Lucifer's semi-spherical chamber lay cold and damp, the torches along the walls unlit for centuries. Lucifer hovered in a transe above his pointed, black, stone throne, putting forth what little strength he had gathered thus far to watch the chaos breaking out on the surface world. He felt joy run through him as he saw every move made from each side of the battle, feeling his strength slowly increase with each descending soul. *I'm not yet ready to face the Four,* he thought to himself. *Just as I gain strength, it appears they are as well. It is a race against time it seems.*

Suddenly, the doors to his chamber opened. A cloaked figure walked in at a confident pace, a serpentine tongue protruding from underneath the hood and black claws growing forth from sandy-colored, scaly skin. The tension in his muscles became apparent as he pulled his hood down and knelt at the foot of the steps leading to the jagged throne. He murmured, "Sir," a little fearful of what would come next from this Supreme Being.

It was then Lucifer's trance-like state was broken. He opened his red, glowing eyes and lowered himself into his throne. He stared at Dante. In a foreboding voice came the words, "You had best have a good reason to disturb me at such a time as this."

"My . . . My apologies to you, your greatness." Dante diverted his eyes from his master.

"Shut up, you fool," he exclaimed, slamming his right fist down, "and get up off the ground, you pitiful excuse of a servant!" Dante quickly rose, looking up at his master now as Lucifer leaned forward in his seat, yellowed teeth gritted and glaring from the snow-white face of the Devil. "Give me one good reason why I shouldn't rip you apart limb by limb right here and right now," he continued, standing up from his throne, his full musculature and eight-foot height apparent. He walked to Dante and lifted him off his feet. Dante began to choke.

"Your highness, I again apologize for disturbing you, but I have important news." Intrigued, Lucifer dropped him to the ground and slammed his chamber doors shut.

Lucifer sat back on his throne. "This had better be good."

"Your highness, Artaxerxes has partially awakened the Four. We have determined they are currently heading to an island just a couple hundred feet off the eastern Michigan coast, where the one called Duke used to live. The island has been completely deserted by all forms of life due to the destruction he caused. At the rate they are traveling, they are bound to be there in the next five minutes. Now, they are not fully awakened, yet. They are still weak in comparison to your greatness, or even to me. Should we set some traps for their arrival, taking them out of the picture now and forever?"

Lucifer got up from his throne and began to pace back and forth in front of the top step. He eventually stopped after a moment or two, his eyes closed. "No," he finally said. "Set no traps for their arrival. Let them be for now. They don't even know of our existence yet. So, they are of no more a threat to us than they are to themselves and to one another." He opened his eyes and turned to the scaly servant. "Is there anything else?"

"No, sir, nothing"

Lucifer sat back down. "Then leave me." Shaking, Dante quickly ran for the doors, shutting them behind him. *I have a challenge ahead,* Lucifer thought as he put his head in his hands. *I have never said "no" to a good challenge. Why, I even tried to beat Artaxerxes with the creation of Hell. However, I still lost. May He someday fall by my hand, for that's the only thing He deserves in this eternity. Then, darkness can reign supreme over all the universes for the rest of eternity.* Satisfied by the thought, he began to hover again and fell once again into a trance.

—∘∘❧❀❧∘∘—

The Four eventually reached Grosse Ile. From where they flew, it was obvious nothing lived there anymore. Where once there were trees, what looked like charred poles remained. Houses sat abandoned, blackened glass and burned stone strewn about. No sound of birds, bugs, or any other animal came from the land. All life was dead.

The Four soon reached what used to be the high school and landed in the parking lot in front. Duke looked around to soak in the sight of what used to feel like a safe haven for him. He took in a deep breath, as if breathing would do anything for the dump they stood before. "It's not much," he said, "but until we find something better, this will have to do."

"Explain to me how this is a 'safe place,'" Lia inquired.

He turned toward her, frowning. "This place has been abandoned for years. After they put the fires out, the place was left to sit here, lifeless. The roads here were blocked off, and the bridges were permanently closed. So, there aren't any cops on the streets. So long as we stay inside, any planes or choppers overhead won't spot us, and we're far enough inland that any cops on the river won't see us, so long as we fly low and stay out of sight if we *do* need to leave."

"It's not much, but I say we go with it," Virgil agreed. "No use fretting over where to hide so long as we can hide."

"Who'd think to look for us here?" Aria added.

"Alright," Lia said, sighing. "Do we all get our own separate rooms then?"

Duke looked away, not having thought about that. "I was just going to use one of the locker rooms in the gym," he answered, looking back over at her. "If there are choppers in the air, there are no windows for the lights to shine in, and there are deadbolts on the doors, allowing us to prevent anyone who does wander onto the island from getting to us."

"Makes sense that we use it, then," Aria said. "As much as I don't like agreeing with Duke so much, these are all valid points."

"Yes," Virgil agreed.

"If you wish to have your own room, though," Duke said to Lia, "I suppose we can't stop you from having your privacy."

"Duke, we've lived together for at least two years," Lia corrected. "There's nothing we haven't seen the others do, and there isn't an inch of any of the others' bodies we haven't seen. 'Privacy' is just a spelling word at this point."

"Then it's settled," he confirmed. "Follow me inside." He waved them after him, walking up to the entrance in front of what used to be the offices, and turning left down the blackened halls toward the only doors without windows on or around them: the gym.

The doors to the gym came off the weakened hinges with a simple pull, falling to the ground. Stepping over the flattened door, the Four entered, looking around at the ashes of those not fortunate enough to have gotten out of the fire, shadows cast against walls, bleachers, and even the floor. They all walked to the door to the girl's locker room, and all but Duke walked through. Duke hung back, leaning against the wall and seeing the remains of innocent victims.

Noticing Duke's absence, Lia walked back out into the gym, finding him staring at the empty space. "Something on your mind, hot head?" she asked, leaning against the wall next to him.

He looked over at her and looked back, spitting on the floor. "Why do you care?"

"I can see that twinkle in your eye," she said, a frown on her face, the genuine sound of concern in her voice. "You play yourself off as not caring for what you did, but you lost friends that night, didn't you?"

He let out a sigh, wiping away a tear. "There was a basketball game that night. The town loved to come support the varsity teams of every sport. It was a rivalry game, and the stands were packed. One of my friends, Zak, was on the team. Many others were sitting in the stands, rooting him on. I had stayed home because I was in one of my usual funks and I didn't want to ruin their night. They knew the drill, didn't think anything of it. Then, it happened." He let out a sigh. "They didn't stand a chance." He slid down the wall, hands holding his head between his knees. "They didn't stand a chance."

Lia knelt down by him. "You couldn't have known that would happen," she said, placing her hand on his shoulder, expecting him to shake it off or push it away, but he didn't. Rather, he leaned back and placed his right hand on top of hers, squeezing it. "We all lost friends the night of our 'episodes,'" she continued. "None of us could have known that what happened would happen." She also let out a sigh, looking at the ground. "The guilt is real, and I know I feel a great guilt when I think about what I did."

"That sinkhole took my family and a couple of my friends," Virgil interjected, stepping out through the partially-opened door. He sat down on the other side of Duke. "Guilt sucks."

"And we've all been bottling up that guilt for a couple years now, trying to pretend like it doesn't affect us," Aria finished, stepping out and crossing her legs in front of the other three.

"Were you two eavesdropping?" Lia asked, a slight smile on her face.

"There are only four of us," Aria said. "If half of us are missing, it's kind of obvious."

"We heard you talking, and we didn't want to interrupt, at least not just yet," Virgil added. "It seemed like we could both relate, though, and thought this is a conversation we should all be a part of."

"Seriously, though," Lia said, looking back at Duke, "they have a point. We've all been hiding our guilt, trying to be these 'tough kids' for at least two years now, keeping our feelings to ourselves, feeling we couldn't trust anyone." She paused. "Perhaps that's what we need to do: trust each other."

Duke let out a sigh. "I suppose so," he agreed, raising his eyebrows. "Plus, we have nothing else to do until Artaxerxes shows up, again. Perhaps this is what we should do for the time being: be each other's support group, maybe even get to know each other a little better."

"Group hug!" Aria shouted, diving and pulling everyone in. While there was some initial resistance, it seemed to relax after the first second, and pretty soon, they were all sitting or lying on the ground, telling stories and laughing as the Sun started to go down.

MAKING THE MOST OF IT

The air lay heavy in the girl's restroom, weighed down by the smell of burnt wood and metal. The door of the room opened, and in walked the Four, their eyes beholding lockers and benches tipped over, smoke stains on the walls and floor, cracked floor tiles all around. They found four benches arranged somewhat in a square. Checking for stability, they sat down, still separated, but yet closer than they would have in the past, as if some strange force was bringing them together. They sat in silence, not even so much as breathing deeply.

Aria, after a few moments, blew the doors open with an intense wind and aired the room out, the smells dissipating until they were gone. No one acknowledged the wind or dissipation of scent, though, remaining statuesque.

After another minute or two, Duke began to notice what sounded like crying. He lifted his head and began looking around, eyes squinted as if to try and see some invisible person. He finally asked, "Do you guys hear anything?"

"Only you talking," Virgil replied, going from a sitting position to laying across the bench.

"Should we be hearing something else?" Aria inquired, looking up at him, an eyebrow raised.

"I hear . . . sobbing, or something *like* sobbing . . . or maybe . . . hissing?"

"I don't hear anything," Virgil said.

Duke continued to listen. "I hear sobbing, like there's someone else here." Hearing the others move as muscles tensed, tensing himself, he walked around, searching high and low for the source of the sound. He soon came to the shower room, and as he got there, it got louder. He stepped into the doorway, and as he did, what looked like a cloaked figure looked up at him and disappeared just as quickly as Duke saw it, or thought he saw it. He shook his head, convinced it wasn't really there. In the far back corner where the supposed figure had been, he found a broken pipe. "Maybe not," he shouted. "Just a broken pipe." He heard sighs of relief as he walked back there, held the pipe together and melted the ends together.

"Told you it was nothing," Virgil commented as Duke sat back down on a bench. "Good to know this place has running water, though."

"Still feels like someone else is here," he murmured, looking around for the cloaked figure he thought he'd seen. "Maybe I'm just crazy."

"Maybe you need sleep," Lia commented, laying down on her bench and closing his eyes. "It's been a long day for all of us."

"Maybe you're right," he replied. "Maybe we all need a little R&R." He laid down on the bench, Aria following suit, the Four nodding off as the last bit of sunlight left the room.

The next day, they awoke to sunlight returned through the windows, shining down on the charred landscape around the school, meeting the eerie silence of Grosse Ile. No one really said anything, merely fixing the floors, turning lockers and benches upright and scraping off ashen coats. What little clothes they found in the lockers were little more than petrified ash, falling apart at the simplest touch.

As the first full day of hiding drew to a close, stomach rumbles echoed through the locker room and they started to smell each other, opening doors to air out the room.

"We need new outfits," Aria finally voiced, unzipping her shirt partially to cool off.

"Clothes?" Lia retorted from the bench she was on. "What about food and showers?"

"The better question is how are we to get these things?" Virgil corrected. "Everyone knows our faces. If we just go on a shopping spree, the cops will be on us in no time."

"All we need is a shopping mall and a grocery store," Aria stated. She looked over at Duke, who was leaning against one of the walls. "Are there any around here that aren't 24-hour stores?"

"There's one not too far from here," he replied. "Last I knew, it closes around 10 pm. It has plenty of clothing stores and has an electronics store. So, we could get a TV and antenna to keep an eye on how close they are to finding us. If we go after it closes, we avoid causing a ruckus among shoppers."

"There'll still be an alarm system and security there, though," Lia pointed out. "We'd need to cut the power in such a way that they'd need to call someone in to fix it. Unless you know where the power room is, that idea goes down the toilet. Plus, we don't have electricity, meaning a TV and antenna wouldn't do us any good, though a portable radio and batteries would still be plausible."

A silence fell over the room as they considered how to go about making this all work. "There'd be lines running under the ground to the mall, right?" Virgil asked. "If they're under the ground, I could easily snake my way around, cutting all wires without disturbing the surface. They'd have to call in pavers as well as the electric company to fix it. We'd be as good as gold."

"Sounds as good a plan as any," Duke replied. "There's a grocery store across the street now that I think of it. If the electricity gets cut there as well, that fixes our food and soap problem."

"We'd need nonperishable foods only," Aria pointed out. "Like Lia pointed out, we don't have electricity, meaning the fridges and freezers in the cafeteria won't work."

"Electricity," Duke repeated, turning and heading for the back door.

"Wait," Lia called. "Where are you going?"

"The classes that graduated before me raised money to get solar panels for the school. The entire western half of the school's roof is covered with them, and they're all hooked up to essentially one giant battery. When that battery is full, it sends that excess energy to the electrical company. If the system still works, we might be able to get any kind of food we want." He flew out the back door and onto the roof where, by fire light, he found the generator. The directions for rebooting the system were a little charred but easily followed nonetheless. He found the "on-off" lever, pulled it down and pushed it up again with giant thuds, hearing the generator kicking on. He saw the lights from the school turn back on below and quickly flew into the cafeteria, opening one of the freezers to feel a cold rush of air from inside. *Oh, God bless solar power.* He ran back into the locker room. "Problem solved."

"Then who's going grocery shopping and who's going mall raiding?" Virgil asked, a smile on his face.

"We all are," Duke replied before anyone could answer. "No one knows what we would wear better than ourselves. So, we all get our own clothes and towels. We get a TV and antenna from the electronics store as well as a wall mount. The radio idea isn't bad either, in case we do happen to run out of power. We all grab food, drinks, and soaps from the grocery store." He looked around and saw the opposition on their faces. "This is going to take all of us for both parts."

After a brief silence, Lia uttered. "He's right. We need to do this as a team."

"All for one and one for all," Aria stated, a smile across her face.

The Four moved to the back door and took to the air, flying above the clouds to avoid being sighted.

A feeling of anticipation remained in the group as they waited for Artaxerxes to show Himself, but He didn't. Days turned into a week, then two. Each day was spent in that room waiting, but no one complained. They occupied themselves with conversations, some on random subjects, some on what Artaxerxes could want out of them, others as a pseudo support group, and still others talking about the relationships they felt developing.

Every night, they tuned into the news, laughing as they reported an asteroid knocking out power to the mall and the grocery store they hit up, and at how they suspected homeless people in the area. Never once were the Four brought up as suspects in the ongoing investigation of what was being called "The 10 pm Raid." Somehow, they had gotten away with it, though none of them took pleasure in their actions, constantly reassuring each other that "it was a necessary evil."

—∘∘∙❁∙∘∘—

One night, quiet had fallen upon the safe haven. The Four were fast asleep, dreaming of lands where they were free of all convictions and could show their faces.

Slowly, Artaxerxes descended upon the group. Once He set a foot in the center of where they slept, He sent up a blue flame, illuminating the darkness. The Four slowly noticed the light and opened their eyes, and, seeing He was there, quickly sat up.

"I apologize for taking so long, but I had to ensure your faithfulness to me, even after gaining freedom," He stated, a tone of confession and grief in His voice.

Duke looked up at Him. "Are we really that poorly-trusted, sir?" he inquired, a tone of annoyance creeping in. "The least we could do is, as you put it, 'stay loyal' to you." The annoyance was now leaving his voice and being replaced by a tone of comfort and care. "You gave us all these tremendous abilities we never dreamed we could have. You gave us the courage and the will power to get out of the hellhole we were living in. For that, we mean to repay you somehow, and since you seem to have a mission for us, we'll fulfill that mission as repayment for what you've done for us."

"I had to be sure, though. As you know, I have been keeping a close watch on all four of you. With that said, there is one matter I must address which I find of the utmost importance."

"And what might that be?" Virgil inquired, an eyebrow raised and curiosity in his voice. "If it has to do with the 10 pm Raid, we had no other choice. We could have stirred up mayhem if we just waltzed into the stores." He hadn't noticed Artaxerxes motioning for him to relax and be quiet.

Artaxerxes turned around to face Virgil directly. "While I do not approve of such actions as you all took, I understand your reasoning for doing what you did and commend you all on your sensitivity to the situation. So, the good outweighs the bad in this case. I simply assume that such actions are necessary evils, given what the public thinks of you four. Regardless, what I *am* in fact concerned about is what appears to be a budding romance between you all. Your love for your special other risks getting in the way and potentially causing a guaranteed failure at the most crucial moment because your mind will be incorrectly placed."

"I disagree," Duke replied, eyes opening a little wider, having now adjusted to the light. "Our 'romance,' as you call it, has yet to get in any of our ways. As I'm sure you've seen, none of our relationships have even gotten past good-night kisses. Plus, we're all perfectly responsible. We'll remain focused on the matter at hand, whatever it might be. I promise you, and I'm sure I speak on behalf of everyone here." He looked around, the other three nodding their heads in agreement, but in disbelief Duke would stand up to Him as he was doing.

"Hold your tongue, Duke!" He demanded. "If you would rather, I could let you live your life in romance with her so the Devil might then steal everything you hold dear from you, including her, or you can hear me out before speaking out of turn again."

"Very well. I'll listen," he replied. "However, let me ask something before we get to the main objective." He looked up at Artaxerxes, hands folded in front of him. "Granted, this is only the second time we've seen you in person, but you seem unusually easy to irritate all of a sudden. Why is that? It's not the 'romance,' because we all know something as simple as that can't cause that much irritation on its own."

Artaxerxes let out a sigh. "My apologies. Simply put, the matter at hand is of the utmost importance, as is the emphasis that no one lets their mind wander for one second, because that one second is the difference between life and death to all humanity."

"Well, if it's so important, then let's get down to business," Lia commented.

He let another breath go and regained His composure. "The souls that lie within you all, they were made by me long ago to put Lucifer away for all eternity, sealed by the Seven Seals of the Apocalypse. However, due to the sinfulness of humanity, the Seals broke, releasing the spirits within you all and awakening Lucifer."

"So, we need to fight some man with horns and a pitchfork?" Virgil asked. "How hard could that be?"

"I am afraid the Lucifer I speak of isn't the prissy figure you all know from Halloween. He is a very real, very dark, and very dangerous being. Luckily, he is not at full strength yet, and therefore is still dependent on his army of dark beings and fallen angels to do his bidding. However, once he *is* at full strength, he'll step out into the limelight and bring about pure destruction wherever he goes. Even in his weakened physical state, though, he is knowledgeable of my doings as well as yours, for he has been watching you four and myself this entire time."

"How are we to defeat him, then?" Lia asked. "Surely burying him won't work, because he probably doesn't need to breathe, and I'm sensing we wouldn't be able to defeat him, even now."

"Too true," He replied. "To defeat him, you must all become not just simple mages, but gods, fully in control of your powers and aware of all things pertaining to your element. The lighting of a candle, the crashing of a wave, the wind across the world, all of it able to be sensed at a mere whim. The planets aligning will reveal the pathway to Eden, which shall lead you to becoming the deities of your respective elements. Unfortunately, you must wait for the pieces to fall in place."

"How will we know when the planets align?" Duke asked. "Will you be telling us?"

"All shall be revealed in time," Artaxerxes stated, putting a hand up as if to say, "No more questions." "As for the romances," He continued, "they may continue so long as you promise they won't interfere with your mission."

"You have our word," they all agreed as the great being disappeared in a flash of light.

Nothing was really said after that point, all four laying back down to sleep as if nothing had really happened.

PATH TO PARADISE

In the distance, the sound of Dante's footsteps grew as he approached a set of great, black doors. Black knobs with pentagrams intricately carved into them left untouched for days lay beneath the face of a screaming demon set as a massive knocker.

Slowly but surely, he approached the doors, reaching forth one of his scaly and auburn-colored hands, his black nails sharpened to knife-like points lightly tapping as they grabbed a hold of the right-hand knob. He turned it slowly so as to maintain the sense of silence about the hallway. The door slid open, without giving so much as a light squeak in the process.

He slid inside, his form concealed under his long, black cloak. Once inside, he slowly and softly closed the door behind him. Turning, he pulled down his hood to reveal his fear-ridden face.

He looked up, his eyes set upon the hovering muscular form of the Devil. Lucifer's eyes were rolled back in a trance. Dante, dreading what would happen for disturbing his master's trance a second time, took in a breath as if to carefully consider his words. However, before he could begin speaking, a deep and sinister voice emanated from the hovering figure before him. "It's been a while, Dante," he said. Then, the form unrolled his eyes, glowing red down upon him, lowering himself in front of his throne and stood there, his gaze remaining upon Dante, who stood shaking and breathing heavily before him. Slowly, he took steps towards Dante and stared directly into his eyes.

"My . . . My apologies, my Lord. I was busy keeping an eye on the Four," he stated, head shrinking into his shoulders, muscles tightening with each step Lucifer took toward him.

"Oh, were you now?" Lucifer remarked, a set of long, pointed nails outstretched and now lifting him off the ground. "I too have been keeping an eye on them, and now I grow curious as to why you would enter my chamber without permission and have the guts to attempt to wake me to report of something I already know."

"My apologies, my Lord. I was foolish to think you wouldn't have been watching them as well. I merely thought that, given the information they have been given by Artaxerxes, we had best come up with a plan on how to prevent their becoming deities, and who better to create such a plan than the Devil himself?"

Lucifer paused. "I see," he finally muttered to himself, his irritation changing immediately to self-centered glee. He dropped Dante to the ground, scratching his chin. "We need to act fast. We need to get them on our side, if such a thing is possible." He started pacing back and forth in front of Dante.

"Unfortunately, I don't think it is, sir," Dante argued. "They seem very dedicated to Artaxerxes now that He has given them so much. They seem to have even taken a liking to Him from what I can tell."

"Well, we're just going to have to change that, aren't we?" he replied, walking back up the steps to his throne and taking a seat.

"Well, if it's possible, I'd like to be of as much service as I can be, sir."

"Very well, then. Let me think it over and come up with a plan," Lucifer commanded, closing his eyes, searching through his mind for any weaknesses they might possess. A few moments passed, but eventually, Lucifer opened his eyes, a snake-like grin casting fear into Dante again. "I've got an idea, and I've no choice but to have you involved in it."

"Very well, sir. What shall I do then?"

Lucifer stretched out his right hand behind his throne, opening a portal with a great tree on the other side. "One of the joys of being the Devil: I can do whatever I damn-well please." A wicked smile crossed his face as he looked back at Dante, reaching out his right hand, pinching a sheet of paper that appeared out of nowhere. "Get the list that fool has left in Eden, and bring it back here. Leave this note where you find the list. They cannot become deities without the list, and if they want it, they need to come to me." The smile fell from his face. "Now go, and leave me in peace."

"Yes, sir." He took the sheet of paper from Lucifer and slipped through the portal, which closed behind him with a bang.

"Let the fun begin." Lucifer closed his eyes and floated off once more into a trance.

After Artaxerxes' appearance to the Four, time seemed to slow down. Hours felt like days, and days like months. Two weeks of hiding out in the rundown school passed by, not a word from Artaxerxes regarding the planets "aligning" or how to even tell, the Four occupying their time by exploring old classrooms and offices, continuing their support group sessions, working out as they had in their cells at the facility, and otherwise talking about random nothingness.

Finally, on that fourteenth night, while watching the news to see if any breakthroughs in finding them had been made, they got their sign: "This is Jenny Russenbergar, coming to you live from outside our studios. It's not that often that there is a city-mandated 'lights out,' but if you all will look to the beautiful night sky behind me, you'll see a phenomenon that doesn't happen but once in a lifetime: the planets aligning. In the hopes that the people of Detroit will take a break from the media and will observe this rare astronomical event, the mayor has declared tomorrow night a 'no lights' night." The Four all looked at each other, relief for their frustration and impatience finding display in the relaxing of shoulders, color returning to knuckles, and smiles returning to faces.

"Now we just need to figure out what we need to do," Virgil said.

"In other news," the reporter continued, "we bring you a video that is going viral across many platforms of social media." The video showed a bright light atop a mountain. "Recorded earlier today, a strange light from atop Mount Everest has been noted as apparent from both miles away and from the base of the mountain. While there have not yet been reports of aircraft crashing due to the brightness of the light, all aircraft have been told to not come within 25 miles of the mountain range. Some speculate that this light happening just before the aligning of the planets is a sign of something much greater, but many more, when asked, see these two events happening back to back as purely coincidental. Again, this is Jenny Russenbergar reporting to you from outside our studios. Back to you inside, Pat."

"I retract my previous statement," Virgil commented as Duke turned off the TV.

"The top of Mt. Everest," Aria noted, amazed by such a notion.

"And we don't have any warm clothes for such a climb," Lia commented. "While powerful, we are still human. We may not survive the frigid temperatures up top. Plus, we don't even know what is actually up there."

"Unfortunately, we don't have time to prepare," Duke said. "Artaxerxes made it clear that we need to go to Eden to start our journeys to greater power. I can try to create a heat bubble that will deal with the temperatures. However, you all will need to stay close to me to conserve energy. As for what we'll encounter, we'll just have to expect the unexpected and roll with the punches, whatever they might be. Who knows? There might be nothing up there, and it may be purely coincidental. In which case, we can say we made it to the top of Everest, something few have been able to claim, and we keep going."

Virgil let out a sigh. "He's right."

"When do we leave, then?" Lia asked.

"At first light," Aria suggested. They all looked at her, wondering why she would suggest delaying the mission. "If we do face anything up there, we need to do so as soon as possible but we also need to be rested. So, we go to sleep and at first light, we dress and fly, as ready as can be to face what lies ahead." The other three just looked at each other, nodded in agreement, and prepared for bed, not another word said among them.

PUT TO THE TEST

Early the next morning, just as the horizon emitted a pinkish glow, the Four arose as if somehow feeling the Sun rise. They showered and got dressed, not speaking a word to each other as they flew out the back door and above the clouds, flying as fast as possible eastward toward the Himalayas. As they got closer, they saw the light and flew towards it, covering their eyes as they got closer and closer, eventually crashing into the side of the mountain from not seeing it beneath the light.

"To me," Duke called over the freezing howl of wind. The other three quickly ran toward his voice, huddling close as he created a bubble of warm air around them. They climbed the remaining hundred feet or so, eventually getting to the very tip where they found a hole leading down into the mountain. As if knowing what the others were thinking, they jumped in, descending quickly into the mountain.

They met ground in a cavern as far below the surface as they had just been above, the light of Duke's flame the only guide they had. They began walking down a labyrinth, finally getting to a semi-spherical chamber, the torches along the wall illuminating as they stepped in. "That's a pleasant change," Lia commented, feeling the smoothness of the walls as they moved toward a bridge that connected the two halves over what looked to be an endless abyss. Before stepping on the bridge, there was a sign etched on a stone slab. "To those seeking the earthly paradise, four challenges you must complete," Lia read aloud as the others followed along. Just then, a black flame appeared on a candle sitting in the giant door on the other side. The Four, looking at each other as if to ask, "Should we proceed?" began walking towards it, finding another slab on the other side of the bridge. "Challenge 1: Melt that which only burns at highest heat."

"So, I need to burn a candle," Duke said. "Sounds simple enough." He walked up to it and threw flames at the candle, engulfing it for the longest time. He soon let up only to see that the candle still remained unscathed. "What?!" he cried. "How is that possible?"

"It's not an ordinary candle," Lia replied. "The challenge said, 'at highest heat.' It's a black flame right now, meaning that the flame up top is the coolest it can be. I think you need to make it the hottest it can get."

"Which would be what?" Virgil asked.

"A blue flame," Duke remarked. "It's black now. It'll turn red to orange to yellow to white. After that, it will turn bluish. I need to get it a solid blue color, like one of the hottest stars in the sky." He looked around, a look of amazement on the others' faces that he was the one with the answer. "What? I paid attention in school." He looked away from them, focusing his energy on the black flame. It began to flicker as it began to gain color, turning a scarlet color. He felt sweat drip down his brow as the pressure in his head began to rise. As he felt the need to focus more to keep the color changing, he put his hands to his head, both to keep the sweat out of his eyes and because he felt like it somehow helped him focus harder.

Soon enough, the red turned orange, then progressed to a yellow. It felt like a very slow process, the loss of patience helping Duke to push harder and try more. The yellow then progressed to a white, and that's where it stopped. Frustrated and feeling his teeth clenched, he reached a hand out at it. "Just turn blue, damn it!" he shouted, eyes beginning to glow, reaching out the other hand, his hands both clenched and colorless. Sure enough, the flame flickered and began to take on a bluish hue, deepening until it finally reached a sapphire color, a line of melted wax falling down the side.

"It's working, Duke," Aria said, pointing.

"Keep it up," Virgil and Lia both shouted, patting him on the back.

After a few minutes of the candle melting, it soon was gone, and the door rose into the wall, Duke falling to the ground as he gasped for breath. "Here . . . I thought . . . that'd . . . be . . . easy."

"That doesn't seem the case," Lia responded, kneeling by him and rubbing his back. "These challenges seem to be tests to prove our worthiness to gain such power as lies in Eden." She looked up at the others. "We all must anticipate such high levels of stress for our tests as well." She stood up and walked through the doorway, looking around for a slab as the next set of torches lit. "Virgil, will you help Duke?" she asked, walking further down the hallway. Virgil picked up Duke, carrying him on his back toward the next door, where they found Lia looking at what appeared to be a ten-gallon basin of water. "Do you all see a slab with my challenge on it?" she asked.

"No," Aria and Virgil both replied, looking around.

"There isn't one," Duke said, sliding off Virgil's shoulders and sitting against the wall. They all looked back at him, wondering what he meant. "It was written on the wall of the cubby the candle was in." He shook his head a little bit, trying to stand up. "It said something like '1/160th of the elixir of life.'"

"'1/160th?'" Aria repeated. She looked down at the basin of water. "What would 1/160th of ten gallons be?"

"One cup," Lia replied instantly. "Sixteen cups makes a gallon, and like you mentioned, that's probably ten gallons. So, I probably have to compress all that water into a cup, but where do I put it?" As she asked the question, she saw the cup sitting on what looked to be a lever on the opposite wall. "Never mind. Let's get to it."

"Hold on," Virgil sounded, holding up his hands. "Your hint was on the previous door. Shouldn't we see if the hint is on the door here, before it opens?"

Lia raised a finger in opposition, wanting to defeat this challenge, but couldn't deny the logic. She started looking around, eventually seeing it behind the cup. "Resist this Category 10." She stepped back, her hand over her mouth. "I think that's you, Aria, and I think Virgil might have saved our skins."

"How so?" Aria asked.

"Hurricanes are measured in 'categories.' A Category 5 has 150+ mph winds. So, twice that is going to be 300+ mph winds, and had that door opened without us being prepared, we would have been swept off our feet. So, Aria, be ready when that door opens." Seeing Aria turn intently toward the door, both hands extended and both feet firmly planted, Lia turned to the basin of water. *God help me*, she thought to herself as she lifted the water out of the basin, holding it near the ceiling in a giant bubble with one hand and slowly transferring it into the cup with the other. Each time it reached the top, she compressed it as much as she could, filling and compressing like a smooth machine.

Eventually, the water started to feel almost impossible to compress. She felt tempted to give up, but noticed everyone cheering her on. All three of them were counting on her and believed in her. *I must believe in myself like they do*, she thought. So, she pushed forth.

As she tried to get the last two cups to fit, her eyes began to glow, her knuckles and hands colorless from the tension in her muscles, teeth gnashed and cranial veins pulsing. She eventually resolved to hold the water in what looked like a tower, putting her full focus on compression of water. Her other hand quickly turned snow white as well until, finally, the water was all in the cup and the lever began to descend.

As the lever reached the floor, the doors began to open, and a strong wind rushed through, hitting the Four. Aria put up a wall in front of them the full width and height of the tunnel ahead. Without words, they filed behind her, Duke supporting Lia as her head stopped spinning and she regained a normal breathing pattern. They stayed as close together as possible, Aria fighting to keep the wind back, her veins pulsing at the very thought of doing what seemed impossible in the moment.

At three-quarters of the way to the next door, the progress stopped, Aria fighting to just maintain position. *I don't know if I can do it*, she thought to herself.

As if hearing her thought, Virgil immediately cheered, "You can do it, Aria."

"Keep it up," Lia voiced. "We're almost there."

"I believe in you," Duke chanted.

They're counting on me, she thought. *I must* do it. *I have no choice.* She pushed like she never pushed before, eyes glowing, hands and jaw clenched as, after a few moments of groaning, the wall moved, pushing the deadly winds further and further back. As they made progress, they saw no sign of the last challenge, but rather found tiles in the floor, each marked with what looked like an element. The first looked like a drop of water. Lia let go of Duke and knelt on the tile, compressing it. The next was a flame, Duke standing still as his tile met the floor. Third was a circle with random lines; the earth. Virgil stood still, almost losing his balance as the tile descended to the floor. Finally was a tile with a swirl of wind on it, right in front of the door.

As the wind tile met the floor, the door opened, and the wind ceased to blow. Aria fell to the ground, out cold from overexertion. Duke and Lia, feeling more themselves with each passing step, picked her up on their shoulders, carrying her between them. They walked down the path until they met the final door, one which was inscribed "Lift as far above as you are below."

Virgil read it out loud a couple times, hoping he was misunderstanding. "Did you all hate your challenges as much as I'm hating mine?" he asked, looking back at the other three sitting against one of the side walls.

"I can't say I hated it," Duke replied. "I didn't anticipate it being fun, though."

"Though it was my element I was dealing with, I saw it as a test," Lia added. "I had to prove that I was worthy of enter Eden, that I was worthy of becoming stronger with my powers over water." She looked down at Aria, still unconscious next to her. "I would guess Aria would say much the same."

"Well," Virgil said, turning toward his door, "let's hope I'm worthy, then." He put his hands palm-up next to his head, knowing he had to lift all of Everest and all the earth between him and the mountain. As he pushed up with his powers, he instead pushed himself to the ground, making what felt like no progress. He heard Duke and Lia cheering him on behind him, though he couldn't make out what they were saying over the sound of blood pulsing through his ears and head.

After what felt like forever, he stopped hearing them and thought they'd either gotten bored or that he had simply just gone deaf in his concentration. That's when he felt it: a kiss upon his cheek, and Aria's voice whispering clear as day in his ear, "I believe in you." Somehow, that was enough. He felt a sudden rush of power within him as he was able to get one foot out from under him. His eyes began to glow as he got his other foot firmly planted. He watched the door raise inch-by-painful-inch as he slowly stood up, lifting eleven miles of dirt and rock. He eventually got to standing up straight, teeth and hands clenched as he pushed, harder and harder as he lifted his arms higher and higher into the air, lifting the door that last foot or so, the final bit of tunnel illuminating with the torches on the wall. The Four quickly made their way through before Virgil set the mountain down as best he could, the door still seeming to drop with a crash. The weight finally off of him, Virgil fell to his knees, sweat soaking his clothes and forehead, his lungs struggling to regulate breathing again.

"Need some help?" Duke asked, putting Virgil's arm around his neck and helping to lift him to his feet again.

"Thanks, Duke," Virgil said. "I think I'm good, though." He placed his hands on his knees and kept breathing heavy. "Just let me catch my breath, and I'll be good." They waited a few more minutes as his breathing and heartrate returned to normal. "Alright, let's go," he said, standing up and leading the march forward down the hall to a final slab of stone. "You have proven yourselves worthy to enter Paradise. Walk through the portal ahead to find that which you seek."

The Four looked at each other, shrugging as they moved towards what looked to be a circular gateway atop a set of stairs. As the first step was stepped on, the gateway began to glow, an image of a beautiful garden appearing on the other side. Quickly, they ran up the stairs and through the portal to the other side, finding themselves in a place that smelled of honey and lush flowers. All around, they found animals of all shapes, sizes and colors living in harmony. Streams of water so clear as to appear invisible flowed both far and wide. It was neither too hot nor cold, not too bright or dark. In short, it was in every way perfect.

The Four felt at once refreshed and invigorated upon entrance, smiles crossing their faces, amazed such a beautiful place existed.

"Where do we start?" Aria asked.

"The Bible talks about the Tree of Knowledge," Lia said. "If there was to be some kind of secret to be hidden, I'd say it would be in the tree somewhere." She looked around, seeing a tree with leaves of a royal purple color, the trunk a deep golden color, shimmering as if made of the precious metal. "I'm guessing that's it there," she said, pointing toward the oddity some hundred yards away.

The Four approached the tree, seeing a cubby hole about ten feet up. Duke took to the air, reaching his hand inside and pulling out a sheet of paper. "What's it say?" Lia asked.

"You four are too late," Duke read. "The list you're looking for is mine now. If you want it, meet Dante outside your hideout at dawn, and stand by me in the fight against Artaxerxes. Sincerely, L." Teeth gnashed, Duke crumpled it up and burned it into nothing. He landed back on the ground. "Let's go," he waved, letting what little ashes survived be carried away on a gentle breeze.

As if by command, the portal through which they entered flickered, the image of the other side no longer reflecting the end of the final test, but rather the bridge they crossed at the beginning. The Four went back through the portal, back through the labyrinth, up the tunnel to the top of the mountain, and out to the frigid air once more.

As they came out, they witnessed the devastation Virgil's test had wrought upon the surrounding area. Snow, ice, and rock had slid down the mountainside, destroying all basecamps and towns in the surrounding area. The sight triggered memories in all of them, each of them remembering why they were locked away from the world they were currently trying to save.

Without another word, they huddled close and flew back to their hideout. Once they arrived, they all fell onto their benches, continuing the long silence that hung in the air. All of them were trying to think of a way to get the list back and push aside the image of the devastation wrought around Mt. Everest. No one spoke a word until Virgil finally asked, "We're not actually thinking of joining Lucifer, are we?"

"Do you have a better plan?" Duke asked, looking over at him, his chin on his knuckles. "We're not strong enough to defeat him now. The list was supposed to be our way of getting strong enough to kill him. Now, that possibility is out the window, unless we do as he says."

"You can't be serious," Lia gasped, appalled Duke would suggest such a thing.

"It's the only option we have," Duke defended. "I'm open to any other suggestion, no matter how crazy."

"Burst into Hell and try to steal it back?" Aria suggested.

"With the hoard of demons at his disposal?" Virgil questioned. "There's no way that we'd survive a suicide mission like that."

"Let's get a good night's rest, address the issue in the morning," Lia suggested. "After the day we've had, we need freshened minds to come up with a solid plan."

The other three nodded in agreement, simply getting up and getting ready for bed without another word. They all laid down to sleep, Lia, Aria, and Virgil falling right to sleep. Duke on the other hand couldn't let the matter go. It simply was too important to just push aside. So, hoping a bit of fresh air would help him think and come to some kind of resolution to help him sleep, he quietly flew up to the roof and sat behind the chimney to the old chemistry lab.

An hour passed by, no ideas coming to mind, when he finally called to the heavens, "If you have suggestions, please, do tell." Suddenly, a blue light erupted behind him. He turned around to see Artaxerxes standing there. "Well, what do you suggest?"

"You're the leader of the group," He stated, sitting down beside him. "What suggestions do you have?"

"The best idea I have is a double cross." Duke let out a sigh. "Now that I've said that out loud, I have to be crazy. Double crosses only work in the movies, and attempting to do such a thing against the Devil himself . . . there's no way. Plus, that plan is probably no good, thanks to Lucifer watching us."

"Don't worry about him hearing us. I've blocked him from seeing us for the time being, but it won't last long, lest he figure it out. Now, tell me what you mean by 'a double cross.'"

"If I can make Lucifer think that I've joined him, get him to feel like he can trust me, I'll get a hold of the list, and once I have it, I'll make a run for it, bringing it back to the group. They wouldn't be able to know about the plan, though, simply so Lucifer doesn't find out. Them not knowing, they'll think I've actually lost it, and I'll have to apologize."

"If you bring the list back, that will serve as apology enough. Your plan is *very* risky, though, as you've said. If you're found out . . . I dare not think of what he'd do to you. I cannot condone you taking such a risk, even for the greater good."

"What other way is there, though?" Duke asked, turning toward Him and standing up. "Short of going down there and killing him and all his hoard, something we're surely not powerful enough to do yet, this is the only solution that comes to mind."

"Like I said, I cannot condone such risky behavior." He placed a hand on Duke's shoulder, a smile on His face. "However, I did not say that I would try to stop you." He stood up and wrapped His arms around Duke. "I understand why you are doing this, and such noble intentions will hopefully see you through. I will keep your secret safe, and I will keep a watchful eye on you." He pulled Duke back, hands on both shoulders. "Be safe, my child." He faded away in a blue light, gone from sight again.

Now, to figure out a way to get Lucifer to think I've betrayed them, Duke thought to himself. He sat back down, head in his hands as he plotted and planned, finally flying back into the hideout and laying down to rest.

FALLING AWAY

Unable to get much sleep, Duke was awake before the others. He showered and dressed, the others not so much as stirred by the sounds of running water or clothes hitting the floor. As he opened the back door, its hinges creaking, he turned around, whispering, "Please forgive me," to the motionless mounds behind him.

Looking forward once again, he stepped outside, gently closing the door behind him. The light of the Sun was barely breaking the horizon at this point, and as was expected, not a sound was made.

"Don't you just hate the lack of noise?" a voice asked from behind him. Duke whipped around, fire burning above both hands as he saw Dante's scaly form leaning against the wall beside the door. "How I do enjoy the sounds of screams in the morning. To me, screams of agony carry a certain . . . *soothing* nature to them."

"Who are you?" Duke asked, muscles tensed.

"Hey, hey, settle down, tiger." Dante waved his hands in a calming motion, a smirk across his face as Duke relaxed and let the flames die. "The name's Dante, and I'm not here to hurt you. I just want to help you. You want this, right?" Dante pulled a sheet of paper out of his pocket. "You all gotta work for it if you want it." He shoved the paper back in his pocket.

"There is no 'you all.' It's just me."

"No luck convincing the rest of the group?" Dante gave a sad attempt at a puppy-dog face while he walked up to Duke, a head taller but leaning on his knees to stare him in the eyes.

"I didn't try to convince them." Duke spat on the ground. "Why let them get super strong as well when I could just harness all that power for myself, have all the powers of nature at my disposal?"

Dante's eyes lit up. "Sounds like you know what you want in life, like you have desires you're not afraid to pursue at any cost." He stood straight up again, looking down at Duke, his face straight. "You'll have to prove yourself."

"Then tell me what I need to do," Duke said, smiling. "Name it, and it's done."

"Turn them into the cops, and lay waste to Detroit."

"And where should I meet you when this is all done?"

A smile crossed Dante's face once more. "Oh, don't worry about that. If you prove yourself, *we'll* get *you*."

"See you in Hell, then," Duke replied, turning and flying low across the sky toward the Motor City.

The other three awoke to find Duke gone. They looked at each other, no one saying a word, seeing in the others' eyes what they all were thinking: *Duke betrayed us*. None of them wanted to believe it, though. So, silently, they got ready for the day, turned on the TV and watched the news while eating breakfast. That's when they heard it: "This is Jenny Russenbergar, reporting to you live from outside Detroit city limits. The city-wide evacuation called early this morning is still underway with thousands still stranded. The authorities and mayor's office are yet to comment as to why the city was evacuated on such short notice. All roads leading into the city have been rerouted until further notice. We've just been told that all power has been cut to the city as well." Suddenly, there was a giant boom. The camera turned just in time to catch the explosion from the Renaissance Center, all five towers crumbling to the ground. "Did you get that? Please tell me you got that." The camera focused in on the smoke, fire, and dust rising into the sky. "Ladies and gentlemen, you saw it here first. The Ren-Cen has just fallen to the ground." Just then, other buildings began falling as well, one by one creating a giant plume of dust and smoke. The screams of horror erupted out of all the onlookers just before the screen went to color bars.

The TV turned off, and again, the Three all looked at each other, silent but knowing what the others were thinking: *Let's go.* They dropped their food and rushed out the door, flying fast toward the major city up the river from them.

As they reached the waterfront, they saw him: Duke. Landing, Aria swept some of the dust away while Virgil brought the rest of it to the ground and Lia put out some of the fire with the river beside them. When the situation was seemingly under control and they could see better, they stared at Duke, unable to think of what next to say.

"Well, are you going to say something or just stare awkwardly?" Duke finally asked, breaking the silence.

"How could you?" was all Aria could manage.

"The choice was simple. Power and freedom with Lucifer, or limits and orders with Artaxerxes. We all spent three years at least in 'the facility,' ordered around, limited by the glass walls around us and the shackles around our wrists, ankles, and waists. You mean to tell me you want to continue that level of limitation?"

"You think you're free?" Virgil asked. "You think Lucifer will just let you do as you please, that he won't order you around like some pathetic bug beneath his foot?" Not waiting for a response, his rage getting the best of him, he began running at Duke, Lia reaching out and pulling him back by his shirt.

"No, Virgil," she said, letting his shirt go while maintaining her gaze at Duke. "Duke has betrayed us all, which makes me leader of the group now." She turned and looked at them both. "Manage any other fires you find." She turned back to Duke. "Leave *him* to me." Without argument, Virgil and Aria took to the air, leaving Duke and Lia alone. "Please tell me this is a nightmare," she managed, falling to her knees, the tears she had been holding back now breaking free.

"Life doesn't always go the way we want," Duke replied, the smirk disappearing, "but you have to do what's necessary, no matter the cost."

"'What's necessary?!'" she screamed as she shook. "How is any of *this* 'necessary?'" She motioned to the destruction around them.

"Lucifer needed to test me, to see that I was worthy of his trust." He held up a hand to stop her, seeing she was going to reply. "Nothing you say can stop me now, not with the path I'm already on, but know this isn't the last you've seen of me." He turned and flew away, leaving Lia alone in the middle of the street, frozen in sadness, anger, confusion, and for whatever unknown reason, hope.

After finding cops and turning over information about where the other three were hiding out, Duke was thrown into a dark cell, almost the full force protecting him. The clock outside the cell ticked away very loudly as he watched the seconds, minutes, hours go by at a snail's pace. Eventually, whether out of actually being tired or just out of boredom, he fell asleep.

Suddenly, there was a purplish light reflecting off the wall in front of him. He turned over and saw a light coming out of the wall on the opposite side. The clock outside the cell wasn't ticking, hinting to him that time was frozen around him. Walking towards it, he could almost swear he heard his name when he was pulled off his feet, through the light, and landing in a room made of black stone, the heat unbearable. He looked around through squinted eyes, noticing the made bed on one side and the two chairs overlooking what looked to be Hell on the other. Between the chairs was a glass table, a couple glasses and a bottle of some kind of whiskey on it. He heard the door behind him open, and, turning, saw it was Dante, wearing a black cloak and holding another in his hand. "Welcome to Hell," he commented, tossing the cloak at Duke. "Put this on. It'll protect you from the heat until you're powerful enough to withstand it."

Duke whipped the cloak on, feeling a sudden rush of cool and comfort surround him. "Does everyone get one of these?"

"Only those who aren't deities or who aren't hell spawn. I was a special case. I am neither, but, being as loyal to Lucifer as I am, he gave me this skin, which allows me the same comforts as the cloak."

"Then why wear the cloak?"

"Because it's fairly stylish for just being a cloak. Anyway, follow me. Lucifer wants to speak with you. Oh, and this is yours." Dante pulled the piece of paper out of his pocket and handed it to Duke.

Unfolding the sheet of paper, Duke realized that it was written in a dead language. "Do you know what this says?" he asked, turning it sideways and upside down as if it would somehow translate itself.

"Not a clue, but I'm sure Lucifer will give you the gift to read it if you have in fact gained his trust." He motioned down the stairs at the end of the hall. Once there, he pointed to the hole in the wall at the end of the giant dome they were entering. "That leads to Lucifer's chambers. Follow me." Dante began walking, Duke close behind. Within the next couple minutes, they were standing before the doors to Lucifer's chamber, which seemed to open by themselves. They entered, Duke following suit as Dante took a knee and bowed, hearing the doors close behind them. "Master, I present to you Duke, ex-member of the Four and our newest recruit."

"Excellent," the figure on the throne said, standing up.

Duke took a quick glance up and caught a glimpse of a sheet of paper in Lucifer's pocket, this paper seeming to glisten. As he saw Dante still looking at the ground, he quickly bowed his head again, unable to put the image of the shining paper from his mind.

"Rise," he heard Lucifer say. Standing, he looked into the eyes of the Devil himself. "Welcome to my legion, Duke." He crouched down before Duke. "How does it feel to be free?"

"It feels great," Duke said, smiling, hoping his face was believable.

A silence fell between them before Dante whispered, "He's waiting for you to call him 'master.'" He elbowed Duke in the side.

"Sorry. It feels great, *master*."

"A habit you will be quick to learn, I'm sure," Lucifer sneered, turning and walking back to sit on his throne. "Your test is not yet over, worm."

Afraid of what else Lucifer would have him do, he asked through a quivering voice, "What more would you have me do, great dark one?" His eyes, though he kept looking to the ground, kept noticing the paper in Lucifer's pocket, seeming to move as it glistened, but Duke paid it no heed. *It's probably the lighting in here.*

"I've seen you strike fear in the hearts of humans and cause mayhem, but I'm yet to see you take a life. However, at this time, I know not whose you shall take just yet." He waved his hand in a shooing motion, the doors opening behind him. "Return to your room. I'll send Dante with instructions for your next test when I am ready."

"Yes, master." As Duke took to the air to fly back to his room, he glanced once more towards the paper in Lucifer's pocket. Now, there was no denying it was moving, and this sight caused him pause.

"Why are you not leaving?" Lucifer growled. "I've sent you away!" This time, he pointed out the doors. "Now go!" As if hearing Lucifer's command, the paper flew from his pocket and into Duke's outstretched hand. Upon contact, Duke and the paper vanished in a flash of light. "Where is he?!" Lucifer bellowed.

"I don't know, master," Dante replied, falling to the ground.

"Then *find him!*" Lucifer roared, picking up Dante with his mind. "Bring me Duke and that paper, or it's your head!" He threw Dante through the doorway and down the hall, the doors slamming shut behind him. Lucifer then fell into his throne, his rage quickly replaced by worry. *The paper must have sensed Duke and his heart, returning to its rightful owner. Artaxerxes must have made sure I'd never be able to hold onto it for long. Curse you, Artaxerxes!*

Rage and fear built up within Lucifer, compelling him to make a quick glance to see where Duke and the other three were, but he couldn't see them. *Artaxerxes is blocking them from my sight.* Even angrier now, he slammed his fists on the chair, shattering the armrests with effortless force. *I will kill Him if it's the last thing I do, and I'll slaughter every last one of the Four to get to Him if I must. Nothing will stop me from laying waste to Him, of that I swear.*

Blinded by the light, Duke covered his eyes, his hand tightly grasping the paper that had just sought him out. Feeling the light dissipating, he opened his eyes and saw he was in the middle of what looked to be a park. A clear night sky with a full moon hung overhead with trees scattered about here and there. Crickets were chirping and an owl hooted off to his right, but all else was quiet. Soaking in that the paper had sought him out and teleported him to safety, he flattened out the glistening paper. It had the same characters as the other sheet, but as he looked at them, the first line moved as if having a life of its own, turning to English. "I am the bird that never dies and who keeps your planet alive," he read over and over aloud. *Okay, okay, the bird that never dies . . . that's the phoenix, if I remember my mythology. As for keeping the planet alive, perhaps it's not the phoenix that's being talked about, but where it can be found. It would have to reside in a hot place. A hot place that keeps the planet alive . . . the Sun! The phoenix must reside in the Sun somewhere. How do I get there, though?* He looked to the sky and said, "Any ideas?" There was no response. "Really? You're going to make me fly all the way there?" Again, there was no response. *Well, away I go, I suppose.* Taking to the air and creating a giant bubble around him, he flew hard and fast out into the icy cold of space, not knowing how long it would take him or if he'd make it home.

ON THE RUN

The stars shone brighter that night than any before. The Three made no note of it, though. They flew back to their hideout in silence. Peace and order was restored in Detroit, at least for the time being, and at least what could be restored after all the damage had been done. Their minds were filled with thoughts on Duke's betrayal, leaving them inattentive to how slow they were flying back to a place they felt they no longer deserved to call "home."

Soon enough, they reached their "home," cleaned off, and went to bed, all without saying a word. The night was not right for sleep, though. Virgil and Aria fell asleep after countless minutes, maybe even hours. Lia, on the other hand, did not have so much luck. She lay there, trying to fall asleep, but kept awake and alert by all the unanswered questions in her head. *Why do I have such bad luck with my loved ones? Why would Duke do this to us? Why am I hopeful he will return after what he's done? How can I love him still? Is he really gone?* She tossed and turned for what felt like the longest time.

A few hours into the night, she noticed lights outside. Raising herself to a window by the ceiling, she saw giant vans with "SWAT" painted across the side, though they didn't have colored lights going or sirens going. The headlights were somehow dimmed, but perhaps they needed them to navigate the terrain. She landed and ran over to the other two. "Virgil, Aria, wake up!" She violently shook them both. "Get up! Get your stuff!"

"Huh, what?" Aria replied, letting out a huge yawn.

"Yeah, what's the big emergency?" Virgil asked, wiping his eyes.

Lia pointed to the windows overhead. "There are SWAT vans outside the school. Duke turned us in to the cops. We need to go." That kicked them into gear. They both flew to the window, seeing SWAT members lining up, live ammo at the ready, flash and smoke grenades on each of their hips.

"That monster," Virgil spat, pulling the school structure down around them in a hasty move. "The entrances to us are blocked. This should allow us time to pack up our stuff. Let's move." The three of them quickly dressed and packed all their clothes, both dirty and clean, along with soaps and such in duffel bags they had.

While Virgil and Aria weren't looking, Lia threw Duke's stuff in her bag as well, somehow hopeful she wasn't just being naïve. *Please, Duke, come back to us*, she thought, letting out a hard sigh.

"Wait," Aria said, "what are we doing? We have nowhere to go."

"Yes, we do," Lia corrected. "I know someone who might help us, if we're lucky." *At least, I hope she does.*

"Fine," Virgil said, waving at the door. "Lead the way. I'll clear the debris in three . . . two . . . one." There was a sudden crash as the debris exploded out from the door. The Three burst out of the door, dodging grenades and what they hoped were rubber bullets. They flew into the clouds, knowing it would only cover them for so long.

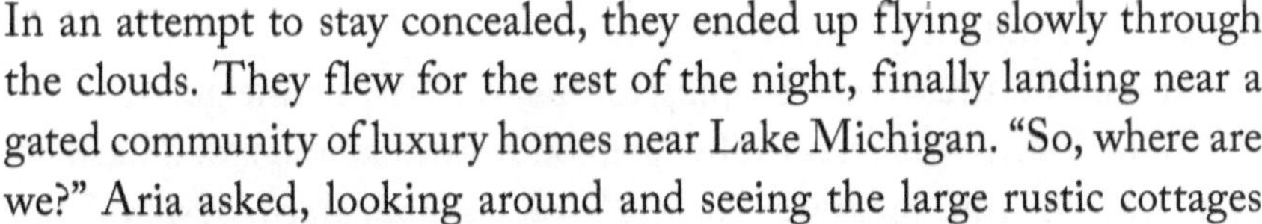

In an attempt to stay concealed, they ended up flying slowly through the clouds. They flew for the rest of the night, finally landing near a gated community of luxury homes near Lake Michigan. "So, where are we?" Aria asked, looking around and seeing the large rustic cottages through the thick trees.

"We're just outside Harbor Springs, MI," Lia replied, walking right up to the gate. "Someone I used to know manages the top real estate agency for this community. I had them tracked down while we were locked up, just in case I needed to find them."

"Who is it?" Virgil asked, looking around and breathing in the pine-scented air.

"You'll see." She quickly flew over the fence and continued walking. "Just follow me, and let me do all the talking."

"And whoever this is will just give us a luxury home or cottage, no down payment, nothing put up as collateral?"

"If the proposition I have for them works out, yes." By this point, they had reached the real estate agency's office, which sat at a split in the entry road. "Like I said, leave the talking to me." She opened the door and walked in. Behind the desk sat a man, typing away on an out-of-date computer. When he saw the door open and realized who it was walking in, he immediately reached for the phone. Seeing this, Lia flew over and smashed the phone. "Don't even think about it," she spat.

"You three are wanted criminals, though," he replied. "We don't serve the likes of *you* here. Please, just leave now." His left hand began to slip under the desk to trip the silent alarm.

Lia quickly yanked him over the desk and pinned him to the floor, hand around his throat. "I'm not taking 'no' for an answer," she demanded, getting within two inches of his face. "I *will* get a home here, and you *won't* stand in my way."

"How do you plan on doing that? By law, knowingly letting you stay here would be 'harboring a criminal.' Therefore, I can't give you a key," he nodded towards the stairway behind her, "and *she* definitely won't give you one."

"Then let me talk to her." She tightened her grip on his throat.

"No," he replied. "She doesn't affiliate with the likes of you."

"Oh, she and I go way back." She tightened her grip slightly. "Let me see her, and I'll be out of your hair."

"Fine," he swallowed, gasping for breath. "Just let me go."

"Good boy." She released her grip on his throat and stood back up. "Oh, and for safe measure, you will want a new alarm system." She reached under the desk and pulled the alarm out, crushing it in her hand and dropping it into the trash. She waved the other two to follow as she began to ascend the stairs.

"Now I *really* want to know who we're going to see," Aria whispered to Virgil as they walked towards a crimson door with gold letters reading "manager."

"Like I said, you'll see," Lia replied as she opened the door, a hint of annoyance in her voice.

Behind the door sat a finely-furnished office, various Italian leather couches and chairs with a couple coffee tables neatly organized in circles, with a desk at the top of a few more steps at the back. At the desk sat a woman of no more than thirty, her golden hair tied back in a bun, and her suit a solid black color. She looked up at the intruders and quickly said to the person on the phone, "I'll have to call you back. Something just came up . . . No, just some unexpected guests . . . Yes, I'll call you right back when I'm done. This won't take long . . . Okay, bye." She hung up the phone and looked back at the Three, then directly at Lia. "And here I thought you were out of my life for good," she sighed. "I'd ask how you found me, but I honestly don't care. What I'd love to know, though, is why you're darkening my doorstep. So, tell me: Why are you here, Eleanor?"

"She used Lia's first name," Virgil whispered to Aria. "This escalated quickly."

"We were wondering if there were any vacant houses available," Lia stated, approaching the desk and ignoring Virgil's comment, "ones that have already been labeled 'a loss,' 'condemned,' or something to that effect."

The woman took off her black-rimmed glasses and laid them down on a stack of papers in front of her. "Why would I ever give *you* of all people anything, **especially** a luxury house in a very fine community such as this?"

"Because it will keep me out of your hair for the rest of your days, and because I'm the daughter that could get you arrested for child neglect." Aria and Virgil quickly looked at each other and back at Lia, both Lia and her mother not looking their way.

"You are no daughter of mine," the woman spat. "You are merely the product of some bad choices in my youth. You caused me to lose all my friends because I suddenly became nothing more than a slut to them. My mother and I were shamed and tormented by that infernal church because of you. My father died in prison because of you. Hell, men *still* won't come close to me because of you; I'm just 'used' to them." She made air quotation marks when she said the word "used." "All this pain, torment, all my bitterness, it's *all* because of *you*." At this point, Lia's mother was standing up, red in the face, and pointing a sharp finger at Lia. After an awkward silence, she put her finger down and let out a sigh, her face returning to her regular flush. "Besides," she continued, sitting back down and leaning back in her chair, "even if that hadn't happened and you were a 'daughter,' I would be knowingly aiding and harboring a criminal. Not only is that illegal, but that's not good for business. So, the answer's 'no.'"

"Damn it, Mom!" Lia shouted. "Haven't you stopped to consider that *child neglect* might be bad for business?" She watched as her mother's face turned white. "Fun fact, Mom: No matter what you say or do, no matter where you go, I *am* your daughter and you *are* my mother." Virgil and Aria just watched as the scene before them played out like a movie scene. "You're my mother, but yet you've never given me *anything* in life! All I ask is this one favor, and you never have to see me again for the rest of your life, ever. You won't hear from me. In fact, I will be so far gone from your life, it will be as if I never existed at all."

Her mother made a little jolt at that notion. She laid back in her chair, twirling a pencil in her hands for a couple minutes, considering the repercussions of such actions. "I never have to hear from or see you again?" she finally asked. Lia nodded affirmatively. A long pause followed as she continued to think it over, but the mother soon replied with, "Very well, you can have the house at the top of the hill. No one wants it because they don't want to drive their nice cars over an unpaved road. Also, the previous owner, a tyrant of a businessman who was hated by everyone in this community, died with no family or friends to claim his possessions. That house may as well have been cursed because it's associated with that man, which deters potential buyers, and without anyone wanting to buy it, there's been no reason to remove the furnishings. So, if you want it, it's all yours." She quickly reached in her drawer and threw the keys to the house out the door. "Now get out of my sight. Oh, and make sure the door hits you hard on the way out." She quickly grabbed her phone and went back to her previous conversation.

"Thanks," Lia replied, waving Virgil and Aria to follow as she exited and closed the door. "Don't say a word," she ordered back to them before they could make a sound, grabbing the keys from off the ground.

They whisked out of the building, flew up the hill, and landed in front of a very large house. It was a two-story home with a round-about at the end of the driveway and a four-car garage just off to the left. They flew up to the front door, unlocked it, and walked in. It was a completely rustic interior, and it was fully furnished, as Lia's mother had promised. There was the exit out the back, leading off to a balcony that overhung the basement exit. A hill went straight down to a river below, trees on either side. Carpeted stone steps led to a balconied upstairs with six or so bedrooms, each with two beds, their own personal bathrooms, a nightstand, two dressers, and a TV with DVR.

The Three walked into this, feeling as if they had stepped into Heaven. "I say we stay here," Virgil said, immediately running upstairs to a bedroom.

"I agree," Aria stated, running upstairs to a separate bedroom as well.

Lia just walked in, not knowing what would come next. *Duke, I have to believe you have your reasons. Please, come back to us.* Dropping her bags at the door, she sank into the couch in the living room and fell asleep.

THE HEART OF A STAR

uke pushed hard as he broke through the Earth's atmosphere, a shooting star in the sky. Breaking the planet's gravitational pull, his "full speed" seemed to exponentially increase. Letting go of his "pushing forth" and focusing now on dodging space debris and maintaining his bubble of air, he found his mind wandering a little, wondering if the Three would ever forgive his actions once they had the list in their hands. He shook his head as if to cast the doubt from his mind. *I have to believe they would see the risk I took for them and, with Artaxerxes confirming my story, forgive me, even if not right away. Who knows what I'll have to do to earn their trust again, but I suppose I'll do what I must. They're my family now, and I don't know what I'd do without them.*

Hours passed, Duke occupying his mind with reminiscing on times shared with the other three and slight disbelief of how far they'd come in just over two years. Growing ever closer to the Sun, he felt its heat intensifying with each inch, his eyesight going dark as he reached Mercury. *Maybe this is part of the trial to become a god*, he thought as he entered the Sun, focusing on maintaining the shield and the temperature within it.

The deeper he went, the more intense he had to focus, his eyes glowing in a sudden rush of power. *I don't know how much more I can keep this up*, he thought as he heard a voice in the back of his mind say, *Keep going straight, you're almost there.* He recognized it as Artaxerxes. Believing what He said, he gave one last push, crashing onto a cool stone floor. He tried to stand up but found himself unable. He opened his eyes, but he saw nothing. It was all darkness, and he realized they had been burned from the light of the Sun. He let his shields fall and tried to move, but every move caused an intense burning sensation. *So, the Sun has not only blinded me but has completely burned me . . . This definitely will pose a challenge.*

:Yes, it most certainly will, he heard a different voice in the back of his mind say. This one was female, and gentle in tone, as if having a calming presence about it.

:What? Who's there?

:I am the one you have come to find, young fire mage. I know why you are here, and I know all that you have done to get here. After so many sins, you took a great risk to come here, and took an ever greater risk to defy the Devil.

:Perhaps they were risks, but I would do anything for my family, even face Lucifer here and now.

:In your state? I did not take you for a fool, but know that I am not one, nor am I without a heart. To your left is a pool of my tears, collected from millennia of seeing humanity tear itself apart. Cast yourself into it with your eyes open, and your sight shall be returned to you. Drink of it, and your strength shall be refilled. Duke felt with his hands, every centimeter of movement excruciating. His hand soon touched something, and the burning on his hands stopped, suddenly feeling wet. With one great thrust, he threw himself into the pool, his eyes open. Instantly, the pain in his eyes melted away and his sight returned. He looked to see the burned, scaly skin that had fallen off of him. He opened his mouth and took a large gulp, feeling his energy replenished. *Now that you are at your full strength, come to me, young mage*, he heard the voice say to him.

He felt the phoenix's presence leave his mind as he got to his feet and walked the labyrinth toward the central room of the temple. He arrived after ten minutes of walking. It was a large dome easily a thousand feet in diameter with four great pillars jutting up in a large square, equally spaced from each other and the walls. Ancient letters much like those on the list were carved into every inch of the walls, ceiling, floor, and pillars. As he looked at them and felt those by the doorway, none changed to English as he had hoped. He continued to look around, knowing neither what to make of it nor the challenge he faced.

As he stepped into the room, he suddenly heard a grinding sound coming from the center of the dome. He stopped and saw a four-foot stone roost rising up from the ground. On it appeared the phoenix. She was six feet tall standing, covered in feathers of reds, golds, and oranges, with blue feathers as the edges of her wings, tail, and off the back of her head. Her beak and feet were black, with knife-like talons protruding. *She's magnificent*, he thought, *and much more glorious than the stories say.*

:Why thank you, the phoenix replied, nodding her head. *Unfortunately, such flattery will not gain you favor in achieving your quest.*

He approached the bird, kneeling and bowing down about five feet away. "The mission Artaxerxes gave me and my friends is too great to refuse. So, I will do whatever it takes to become a god and bring an end to Lucifer."

:You know not what you say, young mage, for there can only be one Deity of Fire. To become the Deity of Fire, as I am now, you must kill me and take my place.

Duke immediately stood and looked up, disbelieving the challenge. "I need to kill you? Impossible. Knowing what it is to be unique, I cannot kill such a unique creature as yourself, not to mention one as beautiful as yourself. Plus, the legends explicitly state that phoenixes never die. How can I possibly kill that which is unable to be killed?"

:Lucifer is a deity, and by definition is unable to be killed, but yet you have accepted such a quest as killing him.

Duke raised a finger to argue, but curled it back, rather saying, "A fair point, but still, why would I want to destroy one as majestic is you? It doesn't feel right."

:I see the hatred of such an act to be true, and I'm honored to see such a change of heart in one who was once so destructive. Such restraint with such a powerful gift as ours is not easily learned, but you have learned it well and therein proven yourself worthy of this fight. She leaned in and pressed her forehead against Duke. *Know this: should you win, I would not hold any grudge against you for your having won. What you must do is a necessary evil if Lucifer is to be stopped. Plus, I have also lived many lifetimes, seen the*

rise and fall of so many a people with my own eyes, shedding tears for so many good people who will never know longevity like you and I. She pulled back and looked down at him, a gleam of sadness in her eyes. *Admittedly, these many millennia have exhausted me so, and I long to rest at last.*

He let out a strong sigh. "What happens if I lose?"

:Then the fight against Lucifer would be lost. While your powers would transfer to an unborn child as they did to you, the wait for that child to learn to use his or her powers would be too long. Lucifer would destroy the world and the other three before it could happen. If you wish to prevent such atrocities from occurring, we must fight to take the other's life, and we must truly seek the other's life for the transfer of power to work. Know that, once the fight starts, there is no turning back. However, the fight is not started, and you are free to walk away and return later, assuming Lucifer has not yet regained his full strength.

If I wait though, Lucifer might become too powerful to beat, and the fight might be lost. We must become gods sooner rather than later. He let out another heavy sigh. *I guess I have no other choice.* "I accept your terms," he said, nodding, fire forming in his hands.

:Then I wish you the best of luck. She unfurled her 25-foot wings and took to the air, the single beat of her wings pelting Duke to the ground. She dove at him, and he quickly flew out of the way as she crashed to the ground, the floor unaffected. He circled around and kicked her head into the ground. She squawked at him as she shook her head. She flew at him, clotheslining him with her wing and throwing him toward the pillar behind him. He pushed off of it, throwing fireballs at the bird as she chased after him. Those that hit the walls didn't faze the stone, and those that hit the bird didn't seem to faze her either.

Suddenly, the bird vanished in a blaze, reappearing in front of him and grasping at him. He attempted to evade, but one of her mighty talons deeply cut his right arm. He let out a yowl of pain as he looked down at the gaping wound. He flexed his fingers, feeling shots of pain but seeing that it wasn't broken. *I need to be more careful,* he thought as the massive bird grabbed him with one of her feet. His arms free, he did the first thing that came to mind and, pulling with all his might, ripped a talon out of the foot seizing him. Screaming in pain, her foot opened and he used this freedom to drag the severed talon down her other leg.

Obviously upset, she caught fire and rammed him into the wall. He put up a shield just in time, saving his spine from certain shattering. He fell to the ground, panting heavily. *I need a new plan*, he thought as he jumped to evade the grasping claws of the phoenix. Now crouching at the base of a pillar, he watched as she flew at him, taking to the air at the last second, causing her to crash into the pillar. He landed on her back and rammed the talon into her spine at the shoulders, pulling it across and severing the spinal cord. She fell paralyzed on the ground.

:A creative move, but I still live, she said, *and I can still vanish and reappear.* At that, she vanished and reappeared just above him, falling and pinning him to the ground. The weight of this heavy bird began to crush him as he felt the air being forced from his lungs. Trying to keep air in his lungs and take quicker breaths he tried to come up with a plan. Quickly seeing he was right below her chest, he moved the talon and jammed it into her heart. She let out the loudest screech yet as she burst into flames and turned to ashes on the ground.

Brushing ash off of him and coughing heavily, he stood up and walked out of the pile, catching his breath, still holding the talon in his hand. *I won*, he thought. *I actually beat her.*

:Not yet, young magi, he heard the voice say. He quickly turned around and saw the ashes recollecting in a giant pile. Then, out of the pile erupted a pillar of fire, which formed into a ball near the ceiling. Once complete, the ball exploded, the force of the explosion knocking Duke to the ground. As he looked up, there in all her majesty was the phoenix, completely healed.

You've gotta be kidding me, he thought, still panting for breath. He narrowly evaded her dive at him, though her snapping beak cut his left calf. He punched her in the eye a few times before she finally got out of line of him. She disappeared and reappeared behind him. Figuring that's where she was going to go, he turned, and as he did, he saw her great foot coming right at his head. Realizing it was too late to evade, he put his hands up, grabbing the foot and throwing the bird to the side. As she was thrown, though, a massive talon came down over his left eye, slashing from forehead to cheek and tearing it out. Enraged at the pain he was in, he felt his power level rise, felt the wounds seemingly cauterize, and began to blitz the bird. Quickly ripping another talon off her foot, he cut one of her wings heavily, each flap a painful squawk from the massive bird. She tried to get away, but she was slowed by the pain in her wing. Duke flew full-force into her, knocking her into a pillar and she fell to the floor. Before she could react, he dug both talons into her back as she tried to take off and ripped through the skin in her back. She fell back to the ground, sliding toward the pedestal. Not giving her a chance to react, he sliced open her chest and cut out her heart.

At that moment, all the letters around the room began to glow, and he saw a tear trickle down the face of the phoenix. *Now you have won, young deity*, she said. *The heart is what keeps a being going. Without mine, I cannot carry on.* Hearing these words, he felt his muscles relax as he dropped the talons to the floor. He walked up to the beast, tear in his eye, and wrapped his arms around her. Her tears ran over the wound on his arm, and it healed. He quickly wiped the tears that had reached his hands and arms over his leg and face. They healed, but his sight in his left eye did not return. He felt the empty hole and the scar on his face, an obvious look of confusion on his face. *My tears can heal wounds, but they cannot replace that which has been lost. Such a wound as yours will be permanent, but it shall be a sign of your battle hard-fought.*

Duke reached his hand up and felt the scar and socket on his face. He let out another hard sigh and pressed his forehead against hers. "I am sorry for what I have done," he whispered, gently stroking her cheek. "How can I make your last moments right?" He pulled back and looked into her eyes.

:Your victory and the promise of Lucifer's demise already has, and fear not, little one, for I will always be with you. Upon those words, she began to glow with the letters. The letters came off the stone, swirling into a great ball of energy above them, the phoenix turning to energy and fusing with it. Once at full capacity, it descended onto Duke, pinning him to the floor and cocooning him, where it then slowly began to fuse with him. For the next half hour or so, he felt his power exponentially increase beyond anything he ever imagined possible. Spells and abilities he never thought of now seemed no more than child's play to him. He sensed all the burning entities in the universe, but only at the back of

his mind so as not to pester him. He felt a burning on his back as what looked to be a tattoo of a phoenix covered the top half of his spine.

Once this was all done, he stood up and looked around. The temple structure began to crack and crumble around him. *It seems the temple cannot stand without the magic inscribed in the stone.* He threw up a spherical shield, soon the only thing left in the core of the Sun. That's when he sensed fires erupting near northern Michigan, noticing a few of the other burning sites he sensed were near the Fours' hometowns. *Dante is looking for me. Best I not keep him or the other three waiting.* With that, he teleported back to Earth.

THE RETURN

The next morning, Lia woke with a start to the sound of pounding and something sizzling. "Keep it down!" came the intense whisper of Aria from the kitchen. "You'll wake her up."

"Well, it isn't my fault that a nice breakfast makes a bit of noise in the process," Virgil's voice returned, whispering but just as intense. "Also, I didn't tell her to sleep on the couch of all places. Besides, if she hasn't woken up yet, we won't need to worry about waking her."

She attempted to fall back asleep, but it was of no use. The noises and the argument were too much to tune out at this point. So she wrapped herself in the blanket on the back of the couch and walked into the kitchen.

When she entered, Aria looked over to see her and punched Virgil in the arm, now yelling, "See! You *did* wake her up!"

"Well, I'm sorry!" he retorted in response, not sounding sorry at all.

"Guys," she started to say, but they didn't hear her. "Guys," still no response. "*Guys!*" Amazingly, even shouting didn't break their argument. She threw water balls on both of them. *That* got their attention. "Will you two *please* stop fighting and listen?" They wiped off the water and nodded "yes." "You didn't wake me. If anything, my body woke me up with how long I had slept." Seeing the grocery bags covering the counters and floor, she asked, "Is there anything left in the grocery store?" They looked at each other, nodding "yes." "Were you seen?"

"I knocked out all the electricity in Petoskey," Aria commented. "Nothing that couldn't be repaired in a day or two."

"And we went in and out through the back door," Virgil added, "away from anyone's view."

"Good. Please, just continue making breakfast. I'm going to go shower and get into some cleaner clothes. I'll be back down in about half an hour or so, but don't wait for me if breakfast gets done before I do." Without waiting for a response, she grabbed the bags from beside the couch she had been sleeping on and walked up the stairs into one of the unoccupied rooms, closing the door behind her.

Once she was finished showering, she got dressed, only to hear shouts downstairs, though she couldn't figure out what was going on. *What are they arguing about now?* she thought as she stepped out onto the balcony. It was then she realized the screams were coming from the television. Pulling the residual water off her hair, she jumped the balcony, landing in the middle of the family room. "What's going on?" she asked Virgil and Aria, who were staring at the screen.

On the screen, a breaking news story was being announced and all three turned their attention towards what the announcer was saying. "This just in. All of Harbor Springs is advised to get into their houses and lock all doors and windows. If possible, the governor has advised a full evacuation. There is what appears to be an army on the way to Harbor Springs with what some are describing as a 'demonic leader' pushing them forward. This army arrives just days after supposed sightings of mysterious creatures in Indiana, near the remains of Santa Barbara, CA, and near Maine's state capital. From what police forces and other news crews have gathered, they appear to be looking for someone or something, though no one knows what or who. Again, it is advised to lock all doors and windows if evacuation is not possible. This is Cynthia Cannicus reporting. Stay tuned for updates."

The TV turned off as all TV stations went to snow. Virgil and Aria slowly turned their heads to stare at Lia.

"All of our hometowns," Aria commented.

"Do you realize what this means?" Virgil pressed.

"That Duke has somehow turned into a demon and is on his way to destroy us," Lia replied. "So much for hiding out here and not being noticed. Let's go." Grabbing a hoodie and pulling the hood up, she ran for the front door and threw on her shoes. She took to the air, Aria and Virgil following close behind.

A few seconds later, they landed in town. People were being plowed by drivers attempting to escape left and right. Police were firing gas cans into the crowd in an attempt to control them, but to no avail. The three of them ran to the center of town, where they heard the army marching ever-closer towards them and felt the vibrations in the ground.

"They're coming!" screamed a boy, running with his arms flailing down the street. "Everybody run to the North! It's the only way out!"

The Three stood their ground, though, the last ones alive in the town altogether. They stood for what felt like no time at all, the sound of unified footsteps growing closer and closer as time moved forward. Soon enough, the army came within sight, stopping half a block away from the Three.

Dante walked down the street towards them. He declared to them, "Lucifer and I have been waiting for this moment for awhile now, and it finally comes. Prepare to fall before the power of darkness!"

"Duke," Lia cried out, "why are you doing this? What do you want?"

"Duke?" Dante repeated. "You think I'm that pitiful little worm?" He began to laugh, and laughter erupted from his army. "Don't make me laugh, sweet child."

Lia looked back at the other two, who shrugged, not knowing who this was either. Lia looked back toward him. "Well, whoever you are, why are you here?"

"We want Duke. Give him to me, and you can live to see another day."

"We don't have him," Virgil called out.

Dante's smile disappeared from his face as his eyes began to glow. "Don't lie to me! He has no one else to go to besides you three. Give him to me!"

"We don't have him, honest," Aria replied.

"Fine. If you won't give him up, I'll take him by force. *Attack!*" The army erupted forward, yelling and waving weapons of all sorts. The Three put up shields and fended off the army, but only just barely. They kicked up gusts, pulled the ground out from beneath them, and threw massive amounts of water from the harbor at them to push them back, but they just got back up and moved forward again.

"It's no use!" Lia cried out. "We hit them but they're unfazed. What are we going to do?"

"Leave them for me," exclaimed a voice coming from above all of them. The army paused their forward movement. Dante and the Three looked up to see a black-hooded figure standing atop a building and looking down at them. The figure jumped down from the roof of the building and landed next to the Three. The figure addressed them, "Head back to the house. I'll meet up with you all in a few minutes."

"Duke?!" Lia blurted, disbelief in her voice.

The figure turned around and pulled his hood down, the robe turning to smoke around him. "Hi, guys." The Three stared at him, obviously wondering what happened to his face and why he was showing his face to them at all. He turned back to the army and Dante. "I'll explain everything when I get back to the house."

"And why should we trust you?" Virgil asked.

Duke held up two fingers, and in it appeared the list. "This is what Lucifer stole from us. Let me into the house when I get done to explain everything, and you all can have it." The list disappeared.

"And how do you plan on doing that?" Aria asked. "The Three of us haven't made any progress as of yet. What makes you think you can do this all on your lonesome?"

Duke snapped his fingers, and the army instantly caught fire, screaming in agony and falling to the ground as charred skeletons within seconds. "Something you all will soon achieve yourselves." He turned his head back towards them. "I'm on your side, and I swear it in the name of Artaxerxes." The other three looked at him with disbelief clearly across their faces, but he knew they were intrigued as to what had happened. They turned and flew away. Duke turned back to Dante now. "Well, you want me? I'm right here."

Dante stepped forward. "So you learned a new trick, so what? You think you can beat me in a battle?"

"It's more than just a new trick." Duke began walking forward, the two of them quickly standing a couple feet from each other, Duke looking up into Dante's figure. "If you think that's all it is, though, have some hits, free of charge." He opened his arms, got on his knees, and craned his neck to look up into Dante's face.

"You must be joking." Dante laughed. "If you insist." Dante slapped him across the face as hard as he could, but Duke just smiled, unfazed. The smile disappeared and Dante raised an eyebrow as he punched him in the empty socket, but Duke just continued to smile. The eyebrow went down and became a frown as Dante kicked him in the stomach and the chin, but Duke still remained unfazed. Lastly, he summoned a sword and slit it across Duke's throat, but not even so much as a scratch. Confused, Dante dropped the sword and took a step back. "What is the meaning of this?"

"My turn," Duke replied, cracking his knuckles and taking a step forward. "Time to see what I can do." He punched Dante in the stomach and watched the towering demon fall to his knees. "Well, that wasn't any fun." Duke kneed him in the face and felt his skull crack. "You have to be able to put up some kind of a fight." Already defeated and trying to escape, Dante tried to teleport away, but Duke put a sphere around him, preventing him from running. "Oh no, you're not chickening out on me. We're just getting started." Duke pulled him up and kicked him in both knees before slamming his palm into his breastbone, shattering it.

"You win," Dante said, quivering and gasping for life on the ground. "I surrender. Isn't that enough?"

Duke knelt by him, running his hand over Dante's scaly skin. "Since you can run back to Lucifer, tell him where we are, and ensure our doom, no." He stood up. "I've become rather merciful since our escape from 'the facility,' but I'll make an exception for you." He held his palm over Dante's face, fire forming below his palm. "You've seen your final sunrise, demon. Don't worry, though. You'll hardly feel a thing." Duke then blasted Dante in the head with a stream of fire. He watched as Dante defended himself with his arms, putting them over his head. It wasn't enough, though.

When the attack was done, Dante let his arms fall, death very obviously about to take him. "Just know that four is not enough to defeat Lucifer," he whispered. With what was left of his strength, he placed a hand on Duke's hand, a purple light glowing beneath it. Feeling an elementary knowledge of dark magic entering him, Duke quickly realized Dante was giving him his powers. As he lifted it, there now sat a purple skull on the back of his right hand. "Use it well." Dante then laid his head back and exhaled his final breath.

Duke held a hand out over the body. The demon's very form turned into solid energy and entered into Duke, becoming a part of him, Dante's knowledge now a part of his knowledge. "Now, to get back to the other three."

"Hold it right there," came a dark and deep voice from behind him. He stopped and looked back. Standing in the center of the crater was Lucifer, his black hair flowing down and his eyes as red and bright as ever. "No one steals my top general from me, Duke," he said. "Give him back."

"No," Duke responded, spitting at Lucifer. "Dante is a part of me now, and *I* will never truly join you."

"How dare you disrespect me?" he screamed. He threw a ball of dark energy at Duke, who deflected it into outer space, never to be seen again.

"He isn't your servant anymore, Lucifer," Duke spat. "He's been freed from your clutches."

"Oh, and the Deity of Fire is going to boss the Deity of Darkness around?" Duke's face turned pale at Lucifer's mention of his position, a look of shock that Lucifer quickly picked up on. "Yes, I know what you have become. Well, let's see if you can command this around." He threw a ball of black fire right at Duke, which he deflected back into Lucifer's face.

"Go back to the hell hole you came from."

Lucifer wiped the single drop of blood from his hairline. "Very well, Duke," he replied. "Just keep in mind that I won't be going any easier on you once I'm at full strength. You will be dead very soon along with your friends, I promise." He descended into the depths of Hell again, but for how long, no one knew. Turning, Duke flew back to the house, not knowing how long he'd be there either.

XVII

THE NEXT STEPS

The front door creaked open, and Virgil immediately lifted Duke off the floor with one hand, pinning him to the wall by the collar of his shirt. "Why did you come back?" he growled.

"Virgil, let him go!" Lia commanded, pulling Virgil's arm down, her eyes sternly pointed towards Duke. "Duke just saved us. He promised us answers and 'the list.' Let him speak." She began to walk from the foyer into the family room.

"You're going to trust the words of a traitor?!" Virgil retorted, letting go of Duke's shirt and following her.

Lia stopped, fists clenched, and looked over her shoulder. "He potentially took a great risk in getting us an item that is our key to defeating Lucifer and saving this world from destruction. He may have betrayed us, but his reason for doing so has earned him a fair hearing." She turned back and walked into the family room. "Sit down and let him talk."

Once the Three were seated on the couches, Duke sitting on the stone hearth to the fireplace, Aria broke the silence. "Start talking."

"Very well," Duke replied, calm and collected. "You all recall we went to Eden and Lucifer had already stolen 'the list' from us." He looked around and saw them nodding. "We were given an option to get it back if we joined Lucifer. I brought that up, but you three seemed opposed to the idea. I needed some kind of a resolution to the issue. I don't understand why it created such an issue for me, but I needed to have a plan. It just seemed too important not to, I guess. So, I sat up on the roof of the school for a few hours, unable to come up with any other plan. Artaxerxes eventually spoke to me, telling me he wouldn't condone such actions, but that he understood my reasoning and would watch over me." He heard Virgil snicker in disbelief but ignored it for the moment. "Dante, the creature commanding the army just now, brought me to Hell after I caused destruction to Detroit and tipped off the cops as to where we were hiding. There, I realized the list Dante had given me was a fake. The real list was kept on Lucifer's person. The paper seemed to sense my presence, flew into my grasp, and teleported me to safety. Once I got back to the room they gave me, I figured out where I needed to go to become a god. That's why I was able to defeat the army and Dante in one easy sweep."

"How did you know where to go?" Lia asked.

Duke summoned the paper and watched as the letters on the first line turned to English, as they had before, and read them the line. "I figured it was talking about the phoenix and that it was in the center of the Sun. So, I flew into space and into the center of the Sun. There, I encountered the temple where the phoenix resided. She explained to me that she and I had to fight to the death for the transfer of power to be successful. During that fight, one of her talons ripped my eye out. Cuts and bruises were healed, but regeneration wasn't a possibility. So, I'm a cyclops now." He ran his fingers over the scar. "Having become a god, I sensed the chaos being created by Dante's army, and, realizing where they were going, I teleported here. After that, I defeated the army and Dante, and he gave me his powers, too." Duke held up his hand and showed the purple skull on his hand. "It's not a lot of knowledge of black magic, but it's enough for the time being." He stood up and set the paper on the table in the middle of the room. "I understand if you all no longer trust me, and I will leave if that is what you all want. Just know that I never meant to hurt you all. I just did what had to be done." He turned and began walking towards the front door.

"Wait," Lia said, grabbing him by the wrist. She paused and let out a sigh. "If what you say is true, we should be thanking you, not condemning you."

"I agree," Aria said, half smiling at Duke. "You took a major risk for the team and for the world, and that is something we cannot hope to repay."

A silence then fell among them, and they all turned to Virgil, who had his head in his hands. After a few moments, he finally lifted his head, and, looking over at Duke, said, "We have all been betrayed, and having you, a person we trusted with our lives, betray us, that was a blow I don't think any of us should forgive." He saw Lia and Aria frown at him, disbelieving he just said that. He held a finger up to pause them as their mouths opened to rebuke him. "However, I also know what it's like to have to make a hard choice and take a risk for those you love." He stood up and walked over to Duke. Wrapping his arms around him, he smiled and said, "Welcome home, Duke." Duke wrapped his arms back around Virgil as the two girls ran up and wrapped their arms around both of them.

The Four were reunited.

"Anyway," Lia said, breaking away from the group hug first, "we should probably figure out our own lines now while we have the chance." She ran back to the couch and picked the sheet of paper up.

"Talk about spoiling the moment," Aria commented as she hopped over the back of the other couch and looked at the paper. Lia smacked her with a pillow, a smile across her face.

"She is right, though," Duke commented. "The sooner you all become gods, the sooner we will be able to take on Lucifer and put an end to his threat." He sat next to Lia. "It only translated my line when I held it. Seeing that Lia's holding it, looks like it's changing for her."

"'I am that which God doth made and you shall find me in the darkest, wet shade,'" Lia read, frowning and pulling her head back. "God made everything. So, that's rather non-specific."

"Mine was a creature," Duke said, "and it was a bird of fire. So, your element is water. Think about sea creatures."

"Okay, there's literally tens of thousands of types of fish, not including sea mammals, certain reptiles, and other sea life. Where do we begin?"

"The phoenix is a mythological creature," Aria added. "So, what kind of mythological sea creatures are there that are God-made?"

A silence fell among them. "The Bible talks about the Leviathan in certain passages," Virgil finally said. "That doesn't really specify what it is in terms of a fish, a snake, or what."

"Well, the physical form it takes is irrelevant," Duke commented. "For the time being, that seems like the most plausible answer to the first part. Now, the second part, 'the darkest, wet shade.'"

"The Marianas Trench," Aria stated. "It's the deepest crevice in the ocean that we know of, and that sounds like a great place for something like the Leviathan to hide out."

"Sounds like a start," Virgil stated. "If that's not right, we'll come back to it." He held out his hand and Lia passed the paper to him. "Let's see what mine says." The words on the fourth line changed to English, reading "The biggest of the Big all would agree, my throne sits within the golden sea." Virgil read it aloud at first, then over and over again in his head. "I've not the slightest clue," he finally admitted, tossing the paper on the table and leaning back.

"Well, land-based and 'the biggest of the Big,'" Aria stated, scratching her chin. "Elephants are the largest land mammal. So, an elephant of some sort?"

"That's possible," Lia confirmed. "I'm not really aware of a mythological elephant, though. The fact that the second 'big' is capitalized bothers me as well. It's almost like that's significant."

"Big cats?" Virgil suggested.

"So, a big cat of some sort, potentially," Lia reiterated. "Maybe a lion of some sort?"

"The Nemean Lion," Duke corrected without a moment's hesitation. "It's one of the animals Hercules supposedly faces as one of his tasks. It's indestructible and vicious." The other three just looked at him with amazement that he could pick that off so easily. "What?" he asked, sensing their disbelief. "I paid attention is school, especially in literature classes." They looked away without another word on the matter.

"Okay, so I have to fight a lion," Virgil summed up. "Where is the Golden Sea, and wouldn't that be a water-based creature then?"

"Not necessarily," Duke said. "What if the sea is made of golden grass?"

"The African savanna then?" Virgil asked. "What would stop a person from finding this creature then?"

"How do you mean?" Aria asked.

"Duke's was at the center of the Sun. Lia's is supposedly at the bottom of the ocean. These are places that are unreachable to humans, at least without very expensive equipment. Mine is just out in the middle of a field of grass, sunning itself on a rock?"

"It's also a divine creature, though," Duke said. "It doesn't need to eat. So, it wouldn't hunt humans or other animals. It would probably remain in seclusion, away from human eyes."

"So, I just have to look all over the savanna, then?"

"Mine was in a temple. All of yours are probably in temples as well. Plus, it's probably a very secluded area of the savanna, without much human life or other animal life."

Virgil let out a sigh. "Well, that's something at least." He picked up the paper and handed it to Aria. "What's your clue?"

Aria took the paper and watched as her letters changed to read, "Both whirlwind maker and fire breather, I lie atop America's ether." She squinted and tilted her head. "A dragon in the Rockies?"

"Yes and no," Lia said. "The dragon portion makes sense, but the Rockies . . . that's just *North* America's ether. The clue only says, 'America.' There are points in the Andes that are higher."

"True. I didn't think of that . . . Mount Aconcagua, it's the highest point in the Andes, and you don't really hear about people scaling it that often."

"Probably because of the dragon up top," Duke said. "Regardless, those are starting points." He stood up and began walking towards the steps. "I'm going to go get settled in. You all go gain divinity, like I know you can."

"Wait," Virgil said, standing up and holding up a finger, frowning. "You're not going to help us?"

"I can't," Duke said, part-way up the steps. "Just as I had to face mine alone, you all must face yours alone in a duel to the death. Only by truly proving yourselves worthy of the power you will obtain will you actually obtain such immense power. Now, I wish you all the best of luck, and know that Artaxerxes will be watching over you." He finished scaling the steps and walked into Lia's room, seeing his clothes hanging out of one of her bags.

The other three just looked at each other, nodded, and, walking to the back balcony, took to the air, unsure if they'd see each other again or in what state, but knowing this was a necessary evil.

XVIII

ROLLING IN THE DEEP

Flooded with fear of what was to come next, Lia reluctantly began flying full speed mostly west though somewhat south to find and destroy the Leviathan. Though she was afraid, she knew she had to face and destroy this "guardian of the seas."

What felt like hours stretched onward, Lia's mind juggling excitement, fear, and wonder all the while. As she reached Hawaii, she created a giant sphere around her and dove into the waters. In an instant, she was immersed in a world unlike what many get to see in their lifetimes. Fish and other aquatic life as far as the eye could see, swimming in and out of coral, mountains, and crevices all placed as if by a master artist. The sight caught her off guard, and she was stunned for a few minutes as she took it all in. In view of such beauty, she felt her fear lessen, though not completely leave. Still, she began her dive deeper and deeper, pushing further down through the water as fast as possible, looking for deeper and deeper points along the way. As she went, she kept a watch out for her target, seeing sunken ships, airship carriers, and even fighter planes, but seeing no sign of her target. *Apparently the Leviathan doesn't leave its nest.*

As she went deeper, she felt the pressure on her sphere increase beyond what she imagined possible and saw the light fade, but she kept going, determined to find this creature. Soon, the light was gone and the pressure became almost too much. That was when she saw it: a blue light deep below. Excited at potentially finding what she was seeking, she swam hard and fast, soon reaching the bottom of the Marianas Trench and seeing the pyramid in all its glory. She swam through the front door, and, feeling the pressure immediately dissipate, she let the shield fall, gasping for breath on hands and knees.

After a few moments, she looked up, seeing the room around her, ending in a hallway lit by more torches. *Torches underwater, there's a combination I wouldn't have thought of.*

:Anything is possible when you are a god, a manly voice said in the back of her mind.

"Who's there?" she called out, looking around but seeing no one.

:It is I, the one you seek. Though a great and booming voice, it sounded almost parental, like it cared for her. *Once you have caught your breath, follow the hallway to me. We will talk more then.*

Alright, she thought to herself. *Looks like there's no turning back now.* Taking a few more deep breaths, she began walking down the hallway, a few minutes later arriving at a room much like the one at the center of the Sun. *This language looks familiar,* she thought, running her fingers over the walls as she realized it was the same letters as was on the List. *The letters aren't changing as I touch them, though.* Just as she thought that, she heard a giant thud and a creaking to her left. She turned, hands up in a defensive manner as she watched the center of the floor open up, revealing a giant pool of water. *This is it, definitely no turning back now.* Then, what looked like a giant tan log floated up to the surface. She lowered her defenses and walked up to it, seeing it must have been at least 200' long and ten feet wide. *How'd a log get down here?*

:I got here by swimming, she heard the voice say as the log opened its sky-blue eyes and turned to look at her.

"Oh my god!" she yelled as she fell to the floor, backing up as quickly as possible. "You're an alligator?!"

:Crocodile technically, he said as he stepped out and began walking towards her. By now she had hit one of the pillars and had nowhere to go. He sniffed her as she shook with fear. *We have not begun yet, young water mage,* he stated, gently rubbing the tip of his snout against her

face, his teeth all-too apparent. *Until you officially declare your desire to take my life, I have no reason to cause you harm.* He walked forward slightly so that his left eye was next to her and looked at her, what looked like a smile on his face. *How can I help alleviate your stress?*

"Help?" she asked. "Well, I hardly know you. Tell me your name."

:Names mean nothing, especially when you are all alone, he said. *Humans give names to each other to distinguish one from another. I am the only one of my kind, which is both gift and curse. I am known by no name besides "the Leviathan." I, however, know your name, Eleanor.*

"You know me?" she asked, frowning and pulling her head back slightly.

:Yes. I am aware of all the water on this planet, both that which moves and that which is frozen. I am aware of your command over it and the things you have done with it, both the good and the bad. I do not wish to try you for your sins though, little one. A guilty conscience causes enough pain as it is. How can I alleviate your fear, though?

"Tell me how to win?" she asked, unsure if that was possible.

:If only I could. I have lived for thousands of years, and you are the first I've seen in all that time besides the fish of the deep. I wish to not be so alone, but alas, such wishes are not granted to those of power. So, to answer your request, that is something you need to discover for yourself, little one. Only then will you prove yourself resourceful and worthy, and only then will I find relief.

Her fear seeming to lessen, she smiled, amazed at how magnificent of a creature he was, and feeling suddenly sorry for him. "Do I really have to kill you?" She half-smiled at the god. "Couldn't I just visit you from time to time?"

She watched him slowly blink, a slight tear falling from his eye. *Unfortunately, to ask such a favor of you would be to doom the world at the hand of Lucifer. So, therefore, yes, death is the only way. Only one deity of water may exist at a time, and you must also prove yourself capable of taking a life should the necessity arise.* His eye opened again. *You and the other three face a great challenge in your future with taking on Lucifer. To take a life is a heavy burden, but necessary in some cases, and know that, if you win, I shall become a part of you.*

She let out a sigh and gently caressed the part of his snout within her reach, a tear rolling down her own face. "Very well," she said, standing up. "I accept the terms of the challenge."

:Very well, he said. Without wasting a moment, he whipped his snout past the pillar and down on the ground where she was standing. She jumped back, springing off the wall and aiming herself at his left eye. He quickly opened his massive jaws, and she narrowly dodged his knife-size teeth as he smashed them down. She knocked his left front foot out from under him and flew towards his tail. Lifting him off the ground by the tip, she threw him into the wall on the opposite side of the dome. As she released, though, the scales on his tail cut her hand wide-open, the first drops of blood dripping on the floor. Distracted at the surprise, she didn't see him quickly get up and run at her. He rammed his snout into her side and sent her flying high and into one of the pillars. She slowed herself down enough where the hit wasn't bone-shattering, but she couldn't stop the hit. She fell towards his gaping jaws, taking flight at the last second and avoiding the snapped jaws. She threw her dripping blood in his eye, and he hissed at her. He ran into the pool and disappeared.

After a couple moments, Lia walked over to the water, and, looking in, saw his immense body flying through the water towards her. She fell back just as he rocketed out of the water and rolled out of the way as he landed, hissing and glaring his massive jaws. *I didn't expect this to be easy, but how the hell do I defeat him?* He snapped his jaws at her. She barely dodged, throwing streams of water at him. He just opened his mouth and drank it all. She tried filling his lungs with water, but that didn't slow him at all. He launched at her, snapping at her. She dodged by rolling into the pool, revealing the bottom half of the sphere. She heard a splash and looked above as he propelled himself toward her. *Apparently this wasn't the best move to make.* She tried swimming past him to the surface, but he slammed her with his tail and knocked her off course. She swam as quickly as possible, trying to stay ahead of him as he sped after her, snapping his jaws.

After a few moments, she quickly turned and got under him. She pushed up with all her might, lifted him out of the water, and threw him into one of the pillars. He got up, seemingly unfazed and launching up at her. She dodged the jaws but went right into the claws. All four claws on his foot slashed her down the front of her torso. She fell to the ground, looking at the blood pouring from her into the pool. *They're not* too *deep, but I can't take any more hits, and I have to end this soon, before I die of blood loss.* She stood up, weak and her mind fading. *I'm about to die. I might as well try killing him from the inside,* she thought, getting into a fetal position and throwing herself into his mouth. As she went, she somehow was able to rip out a tooth as she got swallowed. Holding her breath, she cut through the esophagus, separated lungs and heart from the body, split the spine just below the shoulders, and cut him open through the throat, carrying the heart and lungs with her.

Gasping for breath as she fell to the ground, she let go of the tooth and the organs. Her sight starting to turn to light, she looked at him, blood pouring from his body into the pool. *You did well, young goddess,* she thought she heard him say. He seemed to turn to energy as the letters around the room glowed and formed a ball of energy above her, but she couldn't be sure what she saw and heard was real. All she comprehended though was the light emitted by the energy ball. Once formed, it blasted her with power and knowledge. She lost consciousness as it did.

An hour or so later, she awoke to a pile of rocks resting on top of a shield she didn't remember forming. She looked down, her scars healed, but her clothes still mangled. On her left forearm was what looked to be the tattoo of the Leviathan in all its glory. She smiled, a tear in her eye. *I did it,* she thought to herself as she teleported back to the house. Seeing it was already late afternoon, she seated herself on the couch and let out a breath of relief.

WING-BEATEN

Oh what a day this is turning out to be, Aria thought as she went running out the back door and took to the air. She felt a sudden rush of loneliness running through her, not knowing if she'd ever see the others again. She quickly brushed these thoughts from her mind, honing her focus on getting to the Andes without being spotted.

She flew over the clouds, its cover over the Earth going on for what looked like eternity. Although she didn't see the dragon, she didn't let her guard down, figuring it was probably watching her and hiding out somewhere in the clouds.

After about an hour of flying, she finally reached the Andes. She flew along, looking for higher and higher points in the range, eventually reaching a cave near the top of what could only be Mt. Aconcagua. The air around her was cold and thin, but as she stepped inside, it suddenly felt normal, like she was at the base instead. Not wasting a moment, she proceeded down the hallway and through the winding trail until she reached the central dome. She continued walking, amazed by how much work it must have been to carve all those letters into stone.

:It took no time at all actually, she heard a male voice say in the back of her mind. *Artaxerxes is able to make incredible things simply by willing them into being.* Looking around, she noticed the ceiling opening up,

the sound of stone against stone echoing around the room. She backed away as she saw something rather large flying through the hole toward her. Having landed, she threw up her defenses before this monster of a creature. Covered in golden scales and protruding with spikes on his head and down his back, he stood there, his six massive wings expanding behind his two front legs. Turning his head as if to crack his neck, he laid down as if to nap, his head on his front paws, his snake-like body curling next to him. That's when she noticed the massive claws on each paw and the tips of fangs peeking out from his top lip. *Do not be afraid, young child*, he said after a few moments of staring at each other. *I mean you no harm, not yet anyway.*

Aria lowered her defenses and slowly approached the dragon, gently petting his scales and getting a closer look at his wings. *He must be 150' long with a 50' wingspan.*

:153' long and 48' wingspan, but good guesses, the dragon commented, seeming to snicker. *You were trained well in your homeschooling.*

She paused and looked at him. "You know about my homeschooling?"

:Young Aria, I know all there is to know about you, for I have been keeping a close eye on you from the day you were born. He turned his head toward her, tilting it as if intrigued by her. *I know all that you have done, all that you have said, and I must say that there truly is no one more worthy of obtaining my powers than you.*

Aria felt herself blush. "Well, thank you, sir. I'm pleased to hear you think that." Smiling, she slightly bowed, her hand over her heart.

:You are quite welcome, little mage, he said, nodding at her. *'Tis unfortunate that we cannot be friends and share stories, but there are greater things at stake, as you know all-too-well.*

The smile faded from her face and she let her arms hang at her side again. "Yes, I do." She let out a sigh. "Before we begin, tell me this: should I win, what would you have me do for your final moment?"

The dragon pulled his head back, shocked at the sweetness of such a question, though not surprised she was the one to ask. *Should you win, I ask that you not shed a tear for me. Just let what happens happen, for my powers shall become one with you, and I shall live on through you.*

She nodded her head. "Very well. Let us begin."

:Yes, let's. He quickly unfurled his wings as he slammed one of his paws down with a massive thud. Aria dodged out of the way, throwing a massive gust toward him. He stood and took it, though, flapping his wings and sending an even greater gust than hers in return. She flew behind the nearest pillar as he flew at her. He quickly snaked around and bit at her. She dodged the teeth by flying down, not thinking he'd use his fire-breathing capabilities. Sure enough, though, he breathed fire down on her, her shield barely holding against it. She flew away in a seemingly "cat and mouse" tactic while she formulated a plan.

Finally thinking of something, she snaked around a pillar, ripping out a spike and cutting his top right wing. He let out a massive roar as he regained his balance, breathing fire at her, which she narrowly dodged. Flying up and over, she cut the top right wing again, deepening the wound and nicking the wings below it. As she flew down, though, the dragon turned and slammed his tail into her, sending her flying into the wall behind her and causing her to drop the spike. Not wasting a moment, he raced toward her, but she dodged at the last second, the dragon slamming full force into the wall. He fell to the ground, and as he did, Aria grabbed the upper right wing, ripping it off with all her might. The dragon let out a mighty roar, the soundwaves sending her off-balance. Quickly regaining it, she flew to the ground, grabbed the spike she dropped and ripped a spike out of the wing she had just torn. Now equipped with two spikes, she flew at him, pushing through his gusts and streams of fire until it would be too late for him to dodge. She dipped down, snaked around his body and severed the other right wings. As he began to fall, one of his talons just reached her and cut her across the face from above her left eye to below her right eye.

Worried about the pain of getting blood in her eye, she tried fighting with only one eye. Using her sight impairment to his advantage, he dipped down and around a pillar, out of sight, and his talons cutting through Aria's left leg. She screamed in pain, feeling her anger rise. *Now we end this*, she thought, wiping the blood from above her eye as she found the dragon and flew up and over him at the last second, cutting through all three wings and sending him cascading to the ground. Getting to his feet, he breathed flames up at her, which she pushed aside with her shield and knocked his head into the ground. She took that quick second then to lift him off the ground and throw him into the back wall, where he fell to the ground again. She dove at him, narrowly dodging his jaws.

For the next few minutes, she tried getting close, but his jaws kept preventing her from doing so. *Let's remove the issue then.* Using the spikes, she pushed through the stream of fire and cut off his bottom jaw. Dropping the spikes, she grabbed the severed jaw with all its teeth, and, flipping the dragon on his back, slammed the jaw through the base of his skull and pulled the dragon's head off.

The dragon was defeated.

Dropping the jaw and panting for air, she leaned against the base of the nearest pillar. There, she watched as the letters around her and the dragon's parts formed the ball of energy, which she just sat and took, too tired to resist anymore. She felt the power of the dragon and the knowledge inscribed in the wall flow through her like a gentle breeze.

When it was done, she opened her eyes, seeing the dragon tattoo running the length of her chest and stomach. Realizing it was done, she felt a tear trickle down her face. *I guess that's one promise broken*, she thought, looking around and seeing the cracks forming in the stones around her. *Looks like I need to head home*, she thought as she teleported back to the house, appearing in the family room, where she then saw Lia. She sat down next to her and asked, "You tired, too?"

"Exhausted," Lia replied, "but a goddess." She lifted a hand to give a high five, and Aria tried to give it, but it failed miserably. They both smiled at how bad it was, quietly laughing, but not trying again.

"I hope we don't feel this way all the time."

"You won't," Duke commented from above, leaping over the balcony and landing in front of them. "Your body will regenerate energy soon enough. Between the fight, the powers received, and the knowledge received, though, that's a lot for even a god to handle. So, relax." He then stepped out onto the back balcony, and as he did, he commented, "That, and your high fives won't be as pathetic." He quickly closed the door behind him, expecting them to throw water and air at him, but they just flipped him off, all three of them laughing.

SAHARAN SURPRISE

As he took off, Virgil felt utter fear and loneliness rush over him, knowing he wouldn't be getting help in finishing this fight. All the same, he pushed these emotions aside as best he could, knowing such things would only hinder his ability to come out of this alive. Seeing cloud cover overhead, he flew high and fast, trying to remain undetected as best as possible, occasionally having to dip into the clouds to avoid being sighted by commercial airliners.

Minutes passed, most of what he saw below through breaks in the clouds being water. *I hope Lia's doing alright*, he thought as he spotted land again. As he reached it, he looked around for open fields, seeing the magnificent creatures of the savanna running and skipping about. Though he saw lions, he saw no trace of this monstrous lion. Combing over the savanna from up above, he saw no trace of a cave or a temple anywhere. He soon reached the Sahara without any luck. *A golden sea . . . perhaps it was referring to sand and not grass.* Rejuvenated with hope of finding it, he flew about throughout the desert, feeling himself sweat.

After more time searching, his energy began to deplete and the hope he just had faded from view. The Sun beat down upon him as he flew, the cooling friction of wind on his skin a faint relief. Soon enough, though, he saw what looked to be a large oasis covered in golden grass and tall trees, a large pool of water towards the opposite edge of this sight. Hoping it wasn't a hallucination, he dove into the water, drinking up the cool water as he felt his energy return.

:I was wondering when you would find me, he heard a motherly voice say in the back of his mind. Surprised, he quickly stood up in the pool, looking around for the source of the voice. *Finish your relaxation*, the voice said, *for what lies ahead will most certainly not be relaxing.*

"Where are you?" he shouted. "Show yourself." *And shouldn't that be a male voice, not a female voice? Maybe it's the Nemean Lioness?*

:No need to be defensive, the voice replied, calm and gentle, seeming to ignore his last thought. *I do not eat humans, and you, young earth mage, are too precious to consume.* These words provided no comfort for Virgil as he continued to look around. Soon, he spotted something curious: a pathway leading straight down into a large crevice. At the bottom sat a doorway into what looked to be a cave of sorts. Before he could shout his question, the voice replied, *Yes, that is where I lie. Come to me, child, that we may be able to talk face to face.* With a few deep breaths, he forced himself out of the pool and down the long path into the gorge, the heat at the bottom worse than it was up top. Upon stepping into the cave, though, he felt a sudden relief, almost as if it had a climate of its own.

The path from entrance to central chamber was well-lit by torches along the wall. As Virgil got to the central chamber, he, unlike the other three, took no notice to the writing on the wall, floor, and ceiling, his mind all-too focused on the lioness that lay somewhere in the room, or so he thought.

As he got to the center of the room, looking in every direction, Virgil heard a great "thud" and the scraping of stone on stone. Turning around, he saw two doors at the opposite end of where he entered sliding open. Once open, he saw two large, green eyes open and heard large footsteps approaching him. Out of the secret room stepped an eight-foot-tall *tigress*, her six-foot tail bobbing behind a 12' body. Though she didn't fully extend her claws, there was a metallic gleam every time she stepped. She walked up to Virgil, who stood frozen at the sight of her, sniffed him, and then turned around, laying down between the back two pillars.

:Were you expecting something else? she asked, smiling as she ran her tail along his face.

"Well, um . . ." He paused, not knowing where to begin. "A normal *size?* Yes. Normal *vulnerability?* No. A *tigress?* No. I was told about a Nemean *Lion,* but apparently that's not the case."

:Well, you got the majority of it right, from what I can tell. She yawned, revealing an array of what looked to be metallic teeth. *Before you ask, no, I'm not a robot. My bone, teeth, and claws are harder than diamond, though.*

"Ah," Virgil replied, unsure how he was going to defeat something whose skeletal structure was that solid. "So, like something out of a comic book. Got it."

:My skin is just as indestructible, I should warn you.

"Oh, lovely." Virgil sat against the pillar to the tigress's left and let his head hang, his arms resting on his knees.

:As for the misconception of being a lion, that's easily-explained. When I was young, hunters saw me, didn't have time to register my stripes as anything more than shadows cast through trees and bushes, and they thought they saw a mane on me. So started the legend of the Nemean Lion. I've always been a tigress, though. He thought he saw her smile a little bit. *Regardless, I tell you these things not to intimidate you, little one, but to help you figure out a plan,* the tigress said after a long moment of silence. *If you want to back out of the fight before we've begun, I understand. Just know that Lucifer will not be as merciful.*

Virgil let out a sigh and looked over at the beautiful creature. "You're right. I've just never faced a challenge like this before, and I don't know how one would go about something like this. Plus, the other three aren't here for me to ask them. That is, assuming Lia and Aria are still alive."

:That's the beauty of it, she replied. *You never had to escape a prison before, but you did it on the first try. You never had to escape a hoard of cops and SWAT, but you did that on your first try. You never had to lift all of the earth above you, but you did that on your first try.* She stood up and walked over to Virgil, brushing her silky jowls against him. She then laid down in front of him, eyeing him down. *Virgil, you have done great things in the heat of the moment, things no one else has successfully done before you. You are more than you give yourself credit for, and just as you found a way then, I'm sure you'll find a way now, just as I'm sure you and the other three*

will find a way to put a stop to Lucifer's madness. She then stood up and backed towards the center of the dome. *So, shall we take the first step to putting an end to Lucifer?*

Virgil stood up and, cracking his neck, replied, "Yes, let's." Without missing a beat, the tigress pounced at him, claws fully-extended and teeth glistening in the light. Virgil dodged out of the way at the last second, resulting in the tigress head-butting the pillar. In an attempt to use her disorientation to his advantage, he tried pulling a piece of rock from the floor only to realize that the stone around him wouldn't budge. So, he had just enough time to pull a large pile of rocks out of the walls of the valley outside and down the hall to the doorway. He however was not allowed the chance to attack the tigress with these rocks right then because she had used Virgil's distraction to *her* advantage. Virgil dodged forward at the last minute, lifting and throwing the massive cat into another pillar back-first. He then pulled a large rock from the pile in the doorway through the air and toward the tigress, who merely wacked it with her tail, shattering it into dust. *Well, so much for that tactic.* The tigress launched at him, claws and teeth at the ready. Though Virgil evaded the teeth, the front left claws cut open his left leg. *Time to rethink this,* he thought as he took to the air. She didn't let him, though, digging a claw into his right foot and throwing him into the ground, where she then pounced on Virgil. Virgil caught her by the front teeth and pushed her back just far enough to take to the air.

:Oh no you don't! The tigress jumped between two adjacent pillars, but Virgil dodged, causing her to bounce between the other two back to the ground and jump between pillars again. This time, though, she bounced between all four at random, causing Virgil to lose sight of her until it was too late. As Virgil turned around, the tigress hit him with her paw, throwing him hard into the upper wall and cascading toward the ground, where she was already standing at the ready. Virgil dodged at the last second, the tigress falling off balance as Virgil grabbed her by the tail and twirled her around, slamming her three times into the same pillar before throwing her across the room. The tigress rebounded off the wall, though, launching herself back at Virgil.

There's no stopping this creature, he thought, noticing his attacks hadn't left so much as a scratch on the beast. He caught the tigress by the jaws again, holding them back with all his might until he heard it: the jaw snapped, hanging loose as the tigress backed off, roaring in pain and anger. *The bones can't be broken, but that doesn't stop them from being dislocated. It's a start,* he thought as he launched himself at the feline, grabbing her by the paw and pulling as hard as he could, feeling the front left arm come out of the socket. The tigress fell on that arm, unable to stand straight. Virgil made his way around the beast, pulling on all the legs until the tigress was immobile. He then sat atop the cat's shoulders and leaned on her head. "This means I win, right?"

:*Unfortunately, no,* the tigress replied. *The end is when one of us dies, which, fun fact: tigers have tails.* Virgil hadn't thought to deal with the massive tail which in that moment wrapped itself around his neck and began to strangle him. Virgil tried pulling the tail away as much as possible, but it wouldn't budge. He tried taking to the air to escape the reach of the tail, but that didn't work either. As he struggled, the world slowly got darker. It was in that moment of panic, though, that he noticed the glistening of the front left claws of the tigress. In a last ditch effort, he grabbed the dislocated leg and, flipping the tigress over in the process, bent it between the tigress's back legs and cut the tail off near the base, allowing him to remove it from around his neck. He backed away from the still tigress, stumbling as the blood went rushing back to his head and he regained his balance and breathing. *You still haven't won, though,* the tigress taunted.

"I know," Virgil gasped. He looked around, trying to see if there was something else he could use to defeat the big cat and saw the pile of rocks from before. *She only said her skeleton and hide were unbreakable,* he thought to himself. *Let's see if her orifices are as well.* Pulling small rocks from the pile, he shot them through the tigress's eyes, ears, and nose, all over her insides. Although he didn't get a verbal confirmation, he saw the life leave the tigress as the body fell limp, the tongue fell flat on the ground, and the one eye that still remained attached lost all light. "Now, I win," he said as he fell against the nearest pillar, watching the letters come off the stone and the tigress's body turn to energy, which then blasted him and filled him with knowledge and power beyond anything he thought possible.

When the process had completed, he saw the stone around him beginning to crack and fall inward. So, he teleported outside, thinking he could get a drink of water, but watched as the oasis turned to sand and blew away on a dry, desert wind. *So much for that*, he thought as he teleported back to the house. At that point, the Sun was going down, Lia and Aria were still awake, but only barely, and Duke was standing out on the back porch.

"We did it," he said as he dropped onto the other couch.

"What's your tattoo look like?" Aria asked, looking over at him, not missing a beat.

"Tattoo?" he asked, frowning. "What are you talking about?"

Aria pulled her shirt collar aside, revealing the dragon's marking, and Lia lifted up her left arm, showing the Leviathan tattoo. "Everyone got one," Lia commented. "What's yours look like?"

Curious now, Virgil began looking around and saw what looked like the Nemean Tigress etched onto his right forearm. *How did I not notice that?* he thought to himself. He held it up for the others to see. They frowned at him, wondering why it looked like a tiger and not a lion. "It was a tigress, not a lion," he said. They shrugged and held thumbs up as they laid their heads back and fell asleep, Virgil following suit soon after.

Duke walked in after the Sun went down and, seeing the other three passed out, he smiled and walked up the steps to his room, where he too fell asleep.

XXI

WHAT'S IN A DREAM

Sometime after midnight, frustrated from tossing and turning, and plagued with what he assumed was a nightmare, Duke finally got out of bed and went out onto the back balcony. He stared out into the night, listening to the crickets chirp as the stars glistened from their royal quilt, struggling to make sense of the image he kept seeing in his sleep.

Why is this dream affecting me so? he thought. *I don't understand anything I'm seeing, but it's too graven to be anything more than a dream.* Out of frustration, he threw a fireball into the stream at the bottom of the hill, sending water flying everywhere. *What if it's not a dream, though? What if there's some truth to it?*

"Duke, what're you doing up?" came Lia's voice as she walked out to Duke's side. Standing to his right, she laid her hand on his shoulder, gently stroking it with her thumb. "Having trouble sleeping?"

He crossed his arm over his chest and placed his hand on hers. "I could ask you the same question," he replied, half-smiling as he looked over at her.

"I heard you tossing and turning," she responded, "and I sensed the explosion in the stream out back." She kissed his hand. "Is there something wrong, sweetie?"

Duke looked at the ground and let out a sigh. "That's what I'm trying to figure out." He took his hand away from hers, running it through his hair before leaning against the railing. Without looking over at her, he continued, "It's only been half a day since I absorbed Dante and got his powers, but the thoughts that were in his mind when he became a part of me . . . I guess I just can't tell if they're memories of dreams or pieces of knowledge, and one image in particular keeps coming back to me. I guess I'm trying to figure out if it's a dream, a memory, some kind of fear, or what."

Lia pulled her hand away and rested it against the railing, looking out into the night sky. "I'm here if you want to talk about it." She leaned over and rested her head on his shoulder. "Maybe we can figure it out together."

Duke let out another sigh, gently petting her hair. "It might sound silly, but it's this image of just a black nothingness, darker than anything I've ever seen before, but when I look into it, I sense something in it, something very evil."

"Evil like your father, or evil like Lucifer?" Lia asked.

"Unfortunately, neither. It's something worse than Lucifer hiding in it, something bigger and far more powerful."

Lia shook her head at the thought, almost as if she didn't want to acknowledge the possibility. "Is there anything else besides just that image and that feeling? Shapes? Light or sounds?"

"The name 'Erebus' keeps coming to mind, and I recognize it from my Greek Mythology class in high school. However, I thought it was just that, a myth." He let out a sigh. "I don't know. I can't make sense of it."

"Well, how about anything else? Any indication as to where you were, maybe?"

"That's the funny part: it felt like I was literally everywhere and nowhere, almost like I was between dimensions in some kind of void." He let out a snicker and smiled. "I know how crazy that sounds. It sounds even crazier hearing it out loud," the smile faded, "but . . . I don't know. It just felt too real for my mind to just brush aside as a bad dream."

"So, a great evil, greater than Lucifer, in a void between dimensions . . . Maybe what you're seeing was something Lucifer used to keep Dante in submission, like a mind-control device of sorts. Lucifer tells Dante if he doesn't cooperate and do Lucifer's every whim, Dante gets thrown in this pit with this evil something."

Duke raised his eyebrows. "Perhaps . . . but what if it isn't?"

"Duke," she said, turning him to face her, "I think you're overthinking this. I doubt there's anything more evil than Lucifer. So, for all we know, it's just a manifestation of the darkness within Lucifer. Plus, there's nothing you can do about it until you get more pieces to the puzzle, if there even are any other pieces. So, just take a few deep breaths and go back to sleep. A good night's rest will do you good." She gave him a kiss on the cheek, said, "Sweet dreams, my little fire god," and went back up to her room.

Duke however couldn't let it go. Instead, he continued stargazing for another fifteen minutes, when he finally thought, *Maybe I am overthinking this. Maybe I should just try to get to sleep, or what little bit of it I can get.* He ascended the stairs once more, closing his door behind him.

Once the Four had gotten ready the next morning, they turned on the news, though no one really paid attention. Their minds were too consumed with the thought of finding and defeating Lucifer. No one was really sure it could even be done, given it had never been done before. All the same, they remained hopeful that, with teamwork, their new abilities, and a little luck, Lucifer would fall before them.

After a few hours of the Four spacing out, Artaxerxes appeared before them. The Four took notice to this, quickly sitting up and shutting off the TV. "I sense a tension within each of your minds. So, I thought it best to come here to answer any questions you all may have, since this will be my last chance to talk with you all before the final battle."

"It *will* be your last chance?" Aria asked. "It sounds like you're betting against us, sir. Given how far we've come both in developing our powers and teamwork, that has to count for something."

"Aria," He replied, letting out a heavy sigh, "Lucifer is capable of things you could never hope to imagine. While confidence *is* a good character trait, such high confidence can be a blinder to the reality that lies before you. Don't let your confidence get in the way of your goal, my daughter. Lucifer is an enemy like no other, and he's not one to be belittled. I do have faith in all of your abilities, and I remain ever-hopeful for your victory. However, I am also attentive to Lucifer's merciless nature, his having nothing to lose, and the fact that he is almost at full strength in this very moment. This battle is like none faced before."

"I have a question," Lia chimed in. "How are we to ensure Lucifer doesn't get the remnants of our life energy, our powers, our knowledge, all of that should we die?" Duke, hearing this, clenched his fists and looked down at his feet.

Artaxerxes, sensing Duke's rise in tension, looked towards him. "Duke, I believe you have the answer to this one."

Duke sat up and looked up from his feet. "You all recall how we had to kill gods to become gods, correct?" He looked around at the others, seeing them nodding. "It's the same thing. One of us must deal the killing blow and mean it. Then, their powers, knowledge, memories, everything will become the killer's." Seeing Aria's eyes light up with an idea, Duke quickly added, "Before you all get any ideas though, he's no idiot. He has shields against both light and dark magic set up around him constantly, taking away all options of just snapping his neck, at least before his shields are down for just long enough to knock him unconscious and do so."

"Oh, okay," Aria commented, feeling disappointment overtake her expression.

"Ahem," Artaxerxes sounded, drawing attention back to Himself. "Are there any other questions?" Duke thought to ask about the dream he had last night, feeling Artaxerxes' eyes upon him the longest of the Four. He however decided not to ask anything until further pieces were found. No one else said anything. "Very well, then. I wish you all well on the trial ahead. Sleep well, my children." Artaxerxes ascended out of the house, disappearing from sight.

From there, the Four just sat in the family room in silence. After three hours of silence, they had dinner, eating to their heart's content, not knowing if this would be their last chance or not.

After an hour of dining had passed, everyone felt tired from the spiritually-heavy day. So, Duke said, "You three just head on up to bed. I'll clean up here."

"Don't you want some help?" Lia asked, rubbing his arm. "We can talk about last night some more if you want."

"No," Duke replied, gently stroking her hair and shaking his head. "Like you said, I don't have all the pieces to make any sense out of it. So, I'm just going to brush it aside as best I can until I have more pieces."

"Alright," she replied, half-smiling. "Just know I'm here for you if you want to talk." She kissed him on the cheek and walked up the stairs into her room.

Duke saw the other two looking at him. "I just had some bad dreams last night that bothered me, nothing to worry about," he said. "Now, get some rest you two. We have a big day tomorrow." They flew up the stairs into their respective rooms.

Once all dishes were cleaned up, he stood out on the balcony and watched the sunset for what might have been his last time. After it had set, he walked up the stairs and entered his room, locking the door behind him.

XXII

DESCENDING TO HELL

That night started off as a struggle for all four of them as they fought to calm their minds and relax already-tensed muscles. Eventually, they all got to sleep, though every time they awoke, they had to fight to fall asleep again, a plethora of thoughts rushing back to them like a runaway semi.

When the morning finally came, all four showered and dressed, though no one said a word as they gathered in the family room. No one wanted to admit that this was it: potentially the last moment they would have with everyone alive. "Everyone ready?" Duke finally asked, brushing his hand through his hair, sounding hesitant himself.

The other three looked up at him, no one knowing how to reply. Lia finally said, "I guess I'm as ready as I can be." She let out a sigh. "Given I couldn't think of a way for the four of us to just run away and live alone, unaffected by whatever ungodly wrath Lucifer is sure to unleash if we don't stop him, I'm here, physically at least."

"You were thinking about that, too?" Aria asked, rubbing Lia's shoulder.

"I wouldn't be surprised if everyone did," Duke added, attempting to half smile, though only managing a quarter smile. "That, and just to believe that we're here, about to face the greatest evil the world has ever known."

"Man, why us, though?" Virgil spat, standing up. "What have we done that we deserve to be sentenced to this kind of trial, possibly even execution?" he asked, pointing at himself. "We're barely even adults, and we're facing our deaths!"

"Virgil, sit back down!" Aria ordered, grabbing him by the shirt and yanking him back to the couch. "I'm sure we all feel the same way, feeling punished for something we didn't do." Lia and Duke shook their heads in agreement, though Aria didn't look for confirmation. "Did you ever think that just maybe we're not actually being punished? The souls of the original gods or mages or whatever they were, they could have picked anyone at all, but they *chose* us. I have to believe that powers as divinely-inspired as that wouldn't just pick *anyone*. Maybe it's not what we *have* done, but what we *will* do, like we're the only ones *worthy* of these powers in the whole world."

The other three raised their eyebrows at the impressive explanation, but no one said anything. A silence fell between them for a few minutes before Duke finally said, "Well, no use waiting for the world to end. Let's go." He stood up and waved them to follow him.

"Wait," Aria said as they all stood up, "has anyone thought about what happens when we win?" This question caused everyone to pause. "Our powers were created to take down Lucifer. So, once Lucifer is gone, our purpose in life is done. What happens to us?"

"We go free?" Virgil suggested, obviously unsure. "Job complete, early retirement?" He shrugged. "We could go on our merry ways, staying in contact with one another, or we could stick together and be some gnarly crime-fighting team."

"More likely early retirement of a different sort," Lia commented. "I doubt Artaxerxes would just let us roam the world for the rest of eternity with the abilities we have, even if it was to fight crime or put an end to other evils in the world. He'd probably take us up to Paradise, or at least put us in Eden, forbidding us from entering this world ever again."

"This is assuming we all survive the fight," Aria added.

"All of you, enough," Duke rebuked. "I'm not going to lie, I don't believe that we're all going to die facing Lucifer. Sure, he's the greatest force this world or we specifically have ever seen, but you know what? People said 'the facility' would hold us, but it didn't. People said we're nothing but demons, but we're not. Artaxerxes may have hinted at our not surviving this, but who knows? He may very well just be preparing Himself for welcoming us home as spirits. We don't know what He knows or believes, or how His mind works. Digging too deep into what He says is only going to distract us." They all looked at him, a sudden light in their eyes. "We have accomplished things that no one thought possible. As mages, we defeated gods, taking their places. Now, it's four gods against one god. I like those odds. So, let's go." He waved his hand, opening a portal to Hell. They all stepped through, arriving at the highest ledge in Hell. Looking down, they saw the army beginning to mobilize by the hallway to Lucifer's chamber.

They were expected.

"Okay, listen up, everyone," Duke whispered, looking to both sides of him. "We don't know if any of them have disguised themselves as tortured souls. So, harsh as it may sound, kill anything that moves. Stay together as much as possible, but if we get separated, meet by that passage way on the opposite side." He pointed toward the passage to Lucifer's chamber. No one opposed. "On my mark. One . . . two . . . *three!*" he yelled out as he jumped from the cliff to the grounds below, a ring of fire surrounding their battlefield. The other three followed close behind, landing on either side of him and running straight into battle after him.

The army saw them fall to the ground and began running straight at them, laying waste to everything in their path. The two forces met head on. The Four stayed together as much as they could, walls of fire, water and earth flying up all around them while tornados and random gusts of wind blew the armies off their feet. Some of the tortured screamed out in agony as they were drown, buried or burned in all the violent warfare erupting around them.

The unity the Four had hoped to hold only lasted for a few minutes, though, the army breaking them apart in the hopes of overwhelming them. Seconds after being separated, though, towers of elements exploded from all sides of the battlefield. The army started screaming as their lives were taken one by one.

The battle raged for a while, but the soldiers continually replenished themselves. If one died, the spirit returned, gaining a new body and further enraged. The army never died down and it never got tired, much to the dismay of the Four. It just did not seem to stop for anyone.

:We need to get rid of all of them in one big shot, Aria voiced. *It's like we need to destroy the souls themselves. Maybe if we kill them all in one big swipe, they won't be able to replenish themselves anymore and we can move on to Lucifer himself.*

:While a great idea, Virgil commented, punching one of the soldiers in the face as he threw another in the pit, *there is no one here that's capable of doing that.*

:We don't have to have just one person do it, Duke remarked. *Everyone make your way back to the center of the plain. We get to the center, let them surround us, then force them all into the pit at once.* No one opposed the idea, pushing back towards the center and regrouping, back to each other. "On three; one, two, *three!*" With a giant push, waves of the elements forced the whole army into the pit all at once. Suddenly, they all replenished themselves in full force, angrier than before. They all threw up shields to keep the army back.

"Any other genius plans?" Lia asked sarcastically.

Ignoring her rudeness, Duke said, "Just one." Letting down his shield, he threw a dark fireball at the soldiers in front of him. They fell and didn't return, their very souls burning alive. "So, they can only be killed with dark powers," he explained. "Hold them back for a second. When I tell you to push them in the pit, push as hard as you can." He took to the air, not waiting for a response. He hovered above them, out of the reach of the army, and, extending his hands, eye now glowing, changed the fire in the pits around them to dark fire, the walls now glowing purple. "*Push!*" With one fell swoop, the army was pushed into the pits around them, as were any remaining tortured souls, and none returned.

The army was defeated.

Duke floated back down to the center of the room and gave everyone a pat on the shoulder, smiling, wiping a sweat from his brow. They all patted him on the shoulders as well.

"Where do we go next?" Lia inquired, her smile fading quickly.

"Well," Duke stated, letting out a sigh, "the next direction we have to head is down the hallway I pointed to before." He raised a finger to the only passage that had no apparent lighting.

Without a word, they walked down the hallway. About halfway down the stairway, they were walking in complete darkness. Duke lifted his hand and ignited the torches lining the walls. Their walk slowed as they got closer to the door, nervousness building up in them. Their fate rested behind the doors ahead of them.

After a few minutes of walking down the hall, they reached the largest door any had ever seen. "Are you all ready?" Duke inquired as they reached it.

"How can we possibly be ready to face an enemy of this size?" Lia remarked. "We will always be as ready for him as we are now."

"Good." He let out a deep breath. "Just remember to stay alive. Whatever you do, stay alive." He placed his hand on the upper horn on the left side, opening the door to the chamber.

Everything they had been preparing for was now going to be put to the test, none of them knowing if they were truly prepared or not, or if they would even survive.

XXIII

THE BLACK APPLE

The door slid open to a large chamber, dark aside from eight torches emanating a purplish glow; that of a dark flame. Jagged holes in the wall appeared every now and again from where Dante had been thrown throughout the past years. The Four walked into the room, the door closing behind them on its own. They looked back in surprise, but seeing no one, assumed it was just a slight wind. They surveyed the room around them, fear turning their blood to ice. Their eyes soon met with the steps and the throne atop it, what looked to be a piece of paper taped to the back of it. Feeling their fears fall away at the sight of it, they walked up to the throne. Duke took the sheet of paper. He read it over once in silence before reading it aloud. "'You were too late to keep me from reaching my full potential. Congrats. You have failed.'" He quickly crumpled it up and set it ablaze. "Lucifer has escaped us. All we can do now is go home and pray to catch sight of him somewhere." Without a moment's hesitation, he teleported back to the house.

The other three let out a sigh, hating to accept the truth: they had lost Lucifer, and the Universe was now in grave danger as a result. They teleported back to the house, rage, disbelief, and fear all building up within them.

As they got back to the house, they saw Artaxerxes standing on the balcony, staring off into space. Without even looking back, He stated, "You lost him."

"Yes, sir," Duke replied, his previous feelings quickly replaced by grief. "We will find him, though."

Artaxerxes turned around and looked at the Four. "I just hope it's not too late," He sighed, a definite tone of sadness in His voice. He then disappeared from sight.

The Four sat down in the family room, hoping they would think of a way to find Lucifer.

What felt like hours passed, but no one said anything. Duke got up and went to the outside balcony. The sudden movement snapped the other three back to reality and, seeing his eye glowing in rage, Lia ran over to him, restraining him before he could blow something up. "Duke, relax," she whispered in his ear. "I understand your frustration, but blowing something up or flying away somewhere won't take it away." She felt his muscles relax and relaxed her own hold on him.

"I know," he muttered. "I just can't stand to think we've lost already."

"We *haven't* lost," Virgil commented, walking over. "Just because we don't know how to find Lucifer doesn't mean we won't think of something, and when we do, we'll take him out." He punched his own palm and cracked his knuckles.

"Let's just turn on CNN," Aria remarked from the family room. "If Lucifer appears, they're the ones that'll be first to report it. It's a start anyway."

"I'm willing to give it a shot," Virgil said, seeing the other two agree. They flipped the TV to CNN. After about half an hour, a sudden attack in the Big Apple started playing. In the background was a dark figure standing in the middle of the street, throwing a semi into a distant building before it crumbled to the ground. The camera then zoomed in on the figure as it walked out of the dust cloud, showing Lucifer's glowing red eyes and long black hair atop a ten-foot body of solid muscle.

"To the Big Apple," Duke ordered, standing up. "Meet on top of the Empire State Building." He disappeared, the others following close behind, the real battle about to begin.

———◦◦◦❋◦◦◦———

The streets of NYC went from its normal chaos to a warzone in less than a minute. Once Lucifer had appeared, cars flew every which way like rag dolls, people were ripped from existence, and purple flames erupting from buildings, vehicles, and sewers all around the fleeing civilians.

The Four appeared on the top of the Empire State Building not a moment too soon. They saw the chaos breaking out below them. "Huddle up," Duke ordered after thirty seconds of watching the horror below. "Let me just say, in case I don't get the opportunity later, it has been a true blessing to have known and worked with all of you." They fell into a tight group hug for a second. "However, stay together at all times, and *never* let your guard down. If we stay together and focus our efforts, Lucifer won't stand a chance." Tears began rolling down all their faces. "Good luck," he whispered, pulling away. He then leapt from the edge, blasting Lucifer with streams of fire as he descended ever faster towards the ground. His streams met with a shield of dark energy, reflecting into a building to the side and knocking it to the ground. As the dust cloud erupted, the other three teleported to the street below.

When the dust had settled, Lucifer looked around. "I know you four are here," he hollered. "Show yourselves and I may spare your worthless lives."

"That won't be necessary," came Duke's voice from behind, staring Lucifer down. "It's you who's going to need the spared life." The Four now walked to the middle of the streets, the sound of police sirens approaching from a distance.

"Oh, am I now?" he countered, a grin across his face. "And what makes you so confident?"

"There's four of us and one of you," Aria stated. "You can't defend yourself from everything thrown at you. Plus, everyone has a weakness, and we'll be sure to find yours."

"Such confidence coming from such a shy soul," he remarked. "I wish you four could see the world through my eyes, seeing how the darkness truly does reign supreme with this world, no matter how much any one person pushes it aside. You'd see how futile your goal is, making you all that much more willing to join me and my army."

"We'll never lower ourselves to those standards!" Virgil rebuked. "With the pain and suffering you've caused, you don't deserve anything but eternal sleep."

"Such confidence, for a meat head," he remarked.

"Shut up and fight, coward!" Lia thundered.

"Are we so eager to die?" he inquired, eyebrows raised.

"She has a point, Lucifer," Duke stated, forming fire in his hand. "All you've done so far is talk. Just admit defeat, and we'll take your surrender with pleasure."

"Are you calling *me* weak?" Lucifer pressed, his fists clenching.

"I never said you were weak. Besides, we'd be complimenting you if we did." Duke's smile widened as he noticed how effectively Lucifer's verbal poison was working against him.

"How *dare* you insult me?!" he thundered, his eyes glowing as they rarely had. He threw his right hand forward. A thick ball of purple flames erupted from Lucifer's hand, flying right at the Four.

Duke quickly threw up his hand, the dark fireball growing in size as it reappeared heading right back at Lucifer, who then took control of it and threw it into a nearby building.

"Not bad, boy," Lucifer commented, glaring down at Duke. "It won't matter in the end, though."

"That's where you're wrong," he replied. He turned his head to the other three and snapping his fingers to protect them from dark powers. "I'd like to see your magic work against us now."

"Foolish boy, I don't need to use my magic to kill all of you!" Lucifer picked up a taxicab from the sidewalk nearby and threw it straight at Lia, who sent a stream of water up from the sewage system and repelled it off to the side.

"You're going to have to do better than that," she taunted.

"Very well, then," he said, reappearing before her and throwing a punch at her. She dodged, causing him to fall into a car. It was in that slight moment Virgil picked him up and threw him against the ground. He however got up, unmarked and unaffected. He teleported behind Virgil, picked him up off the ground and slammed him through a building wall. Virgil got up though with only a little redness on his forehead. The world underneath Lucifer then came up in a wave, sending Lucifer to the sky, where he disappeared from sight.

"Where did he go?" Lia implored, worried they had lost him again.

"I am right here, my sweet," he replied as he reappeared behind her, kicking her in the back and smashing her into the pavement, the sound of her ribs shattering echoing off the buildings. She was then picked up and whirled towards a brick wall, but Duke quickly caught her, setting her down in an alley. He threw multiple streams of fire at Lucifer, Lucifer's laughter emanating from within the onslaught of heat. "Do you honestly think that's going to do anything?" he inquired, a dark energy stream hitting Duke from behind and pounding him into the ground, the rain of fire stopped for the moment.

"Did you honestly think *that* was going to do anything?" Duke countered as he got up from the crater, rubbing his right shoulder and wiping the blood from the side of his neck. "The four of us are stronger than you give us credit for being."

"Oh, is that so?" Another dark energy stream came at Duke. However, Duke threw up a hand, redirecting the attack to both sides of him. Duke took to the air and flew at Lucifer. Just as he was about to be knocked out of the air by Lucifer's fist, he dove down and knocked Lucifer's feet out from under him, Lucifer's head smashing into the semi behind him. Lucifer however quickly grabbed Duke and smashed him into the ground, stepping on his upper back to weigh him down and stomping his other foot on Duke's lower back, the sound of his spine breaking echoing off into the distance.

"You're going to regret doing that!" Lia yelled, flying right at him and knocking him clear off his feet again. She landed by Duke's side only to be kicked in the face and sent through the building behind her.

"You bastard!" Aria shouted, a tornado pinning Lucifer to the ground, pushing harder and harder with each second. He however laughed, as if it somehow tickled him. He stretched out a hand and sent forth a stream of dark fire that nailed her in the face, knocking her to the ground and ending the tornado. Once up, he teleported over to her and stomped down on her rib cage.

"You cannot defeat me." He watched Lia limp back into sight, Duke pulling himself off the ground and blasting Lucifer with a stream of fire before running to Aria's side.

Virgil ran over to Aria's side. "Speak to me, Aria," he cried. He looked over at Duke. "Is she going to be okay?"

Looking over Aria's body, analyzing any marks or injuries, he responded with, "She'll be fine in due time. She's unconscious, and I'm guessing her rib cage has been shattered horribly. Once she comes to, she'll heal herself up, like we've been doing so far. However, we have to protect her from losing *more than* her consciousness for the time being."

Virgil looked down at her fractured and motionless body, a tear rolling down his face, rage building within him. "Very well, then," he said, standing up. "I'll hold off Lucifer for the time being. Get her to safety."

"Virgil, no!" Lia countered, dodging a few streams of dark energy as she restrained him. Duke threw up a shield to protect them from the rest of the streams. "You can't risk your life like that," she continued.

"Save Aria," he ordered, standing up and shaking off the restraints. "I have a personal score to settle with him now."

"Virgil, listen to Lia!" Duke ordered. "Don't take him on by yourself!"

"*Go!*" he thundered, lifting the ground underneath them up so they were thrown through the doorway to a building, now blocked by concrete and smashed cars. He turned back to Lucifer. "You're as good as dead now."

"Oh, am I now?" he taunted, a smile on his face, throwing a few dark magic spells at Virgil, all of them being repelled by the shields Duke had set up earlier. "Duke knows his shield structure," he marveled slightly, "but I know it better." Lucifer's fist caught fire as he zipped up to Virgil and punched him in the stomach, shattering both shields. Virgil fell back in pain. "You're a dead man."

"Not yet I'm not!" he remarked, eyes glowing bright green. He began throwing punch after punch at Lucifer, each one deflected. The rapid punches were soon accompanied by kicks, one of them finally landing on Lucifer's jaw. Lucifer fell back, a slight gash on his chin now.

Wiping the blood from his chin and looking at it, he looked up at Virgil, eyes glowing brighter. He threw a punch at Virgil, which was caught, but took both of Virgil's hands and all his strength to hold back, leaving nothing to defend him from Lucifer's other fist, which flew right into Virgil's face, knocking some teeth to the ground a few seconds after he fell. Virgil quickly reappeared right behind Lucifer and kicked him across the head, knocking him to the ground, where Virgil nailed him in the stomach and upwards across his chin with a couple more kicks, knocking a tooth out. However, when he went to punch Lucifer in the face, Lucifer easily grabbed Virgil by the arm and twisted it behind his back. "Now is when you die," he whispered in Virgil's ear.

Suddenly, the concrete and metal fell out of the doorway, Lia and Duke flying through, somewhat recovered. This distracted Lucifer enough to allow Virgil to escape, taking to the air and saying, "I beg to differ." Lucifer however didn't look Virgil's way, looking at Lia and Duke in the doorway. He however didn't need to look Virgil's way, because he could hear Virgil flying up behind him. This was when Lucifer spun around and punched Virgil full-force in the face, Lucifer's fist indenting Virgil's head. Horribly injured, he fell to the ground, where Lucifer then blasted him with a thick stream of dark fire.

"Virgil!" Duke and Lia screamed in almost perfect unison.

Lucifer ceased his attack and looked their way, smirking. "Until next time," they heard him say as he disappeared from sight.

Duke and Lia flew to Virgil's side, tears rolling down their face as they shook his motionless body. "Wake up," Lia said. "Please, wake up." There however was no response.

"You won't have died in vain, Virgil," Duke muttered as he snapped Virgil's neck and held him close. He placed his right hand over Virgil's heart. Virgil's body, life energy, everything that was Virgil flowed into him and became one with Duke. The mark of the Nemean Tigress shown itself on his right arm now.

"We should go after him," Lia commented, taking a stand and beginning to walk back up the street, but stopping when she noticed Duke hadn't moved.

After a few seconds, Duke looked up to her. "We've lost the battle, Lia. One of the Four is dead, and another is unconscious. We have two left able to fight, one of whom is presently doing everything within his power to digest all the knowledge and power becoming a part of him. You'd essentially be taking him on by yourself, and that's too great of a risk." He then looked down at the broken concrete, tears still flowing down his face. "Let's go home."

"What about Lucifer, though? What if he begins another attack in New York City?"

Duke shook his head. "He's gone back to his chamber. He succeeded in doing what he wanted to do: instill fear into the world's population, torment them with their own emotions." He looked down at the tigress on his arm. "This was just a small bonus for him." He looked back up at her. "No, he's done for the day, as we should be as well." He stood up and began walking back to where Aria was resting. Picking her up, he said, "I've got Aria. Meet me in the family room." He disappeared in an instant, Lia following close behind.

Both of them arrived home in an instant. Duke set Aria's body on the couch and walked out back, Lia close behind. There, Duke lifted a large boulder from the river. He formed it into a statue of Virgil and inscribed Virgil's name on the base. "Rest easy, brother," he whispered. Candles around the base lit themselves. Duke fell to his knees, Lia sitting next to him. They both began to cry.

An hour later, Aria woke up, and seeing them, came outside. "What's going on?" she asked, approaching them. "Where's Virgil?" Unable to say anything, Duke pointed at the statue, which Aria immediately froze at the sight of. Her eyes widened, tears rolling down her face instantly as she realized what had happened. "No, anything but that!" she hollered. She fell to her knees and covered her mouth with her hands. "Tell me this is just a dream!"

"I wish it were," Duke muttered, wiping the tears from his face and looking back at Aria while rubbing Lia's back.

"*No!*" she screamed through even heavier sobs. The scream echoed for a good minute to minute and a half. She joined in with Lia and Duke, each one of them comforting the other two to the best of their abilities, though all of them were struck cold by Virgil's death.

They sat there for another hour, going back up to the house afterwards and going to bed, none of them speaking another word the entire time.

Virgil was now dead. They had lost their first battle, making the goal of winning the war that much harder. Regardless, the war had begun. *That* was a certainty.

XXIV

DÍA DE LA MUERTE

That night, none of the Three could sleep, all of them overrun with sadness and anger unlike anything they ever felt. A hole rested in each of their hearts, no matter how much they told themselves or each other he remained in their memories, never to be forgotten. These memories and emotions ended up keeping the Three up the rest of the night.

As the Sun rose on the house, the Three got out of bed and got ready in complete silence. Once ready, they entered the kitchen, poured out a glass of juice and sat at the table, taking a sip every minute or so.

After some time had passed, Artaxerxes descended into the room, hands folded behind His back. "Why do you not hasten on?" He pressed, stepping before them and sitting at the opposite side of the table.

"Would you rather we be trophies on Lucifer's wall?" Aria rebuked.

"You misunderstand my question. Why are you not out looking for him?" His eyes began to glow more intensely.

"We lost one of our only friends yesterday, sir," Duke replied, looking up from the table. "Are you so heartless that we can't have just one day to mourn his sacrifice for us?"

"Duke, you know my heart to be just and loving. If such accommodations could be made, I would. However, Lucifer would take advantage of your 'day of mourning' and surely gain an upper hand. You all have seen both his power and how he wields it. He cannot be allowed such a privilege as to cause further destruction."

"Sir," Aria interjected, "if he's as strong as you make him out to be, and we know his strength now, why is it you are not out fighting at our side?"

He sighed heavily. "If I were to die, and you three didn't succeed, Lucifer would have no opposition left to take him down. In the grand scheme of things, I am but a final measure, to be used once you four are gone and he is severely weakened."

The Three looked at each other, realizing what this meant, but not saying anything aside from, "Very well, then."

"How do you suggest we find him?" Lia inquired. "He could be anywhere."

"What matters is not *how* he is found, just *that* he is found," He replied, disappearing as quickly as he came.

"I can't believe Artaxerxes would push Virgil aside like that," Aria finally commented after a long, heavy silence. "Seriously, it infuriates me!"

"Aria," Duke replied as he turned on the TV, "He more or less just admitted that we are all just pawns in this game of His. We've defeated all of Lucifer's pawns, and now we are free to go for the king like good little knights."

"Duke," Lia rebuked, "this isn't a game of chess, and we're not insignificant pawns." She paused, staring off into space. "We can't be," she added, her voice now softened.

"Okay. Regardless, we are His children, made to do as He wishes, even though we have minds enough to rebel, and He knows that. However, He also knows that He's strong enough to overpower us, and thereby knows we won't rebel." Duke fell silent, falling into a seat in the family room. He closed his eye, his head slouched, as if deep in thought. "Let's go," he suddenly ordered a few seconds later, standing up and heading back into the kitchen.

"Where are we going?" Lia inquired. "We need to find Lucifer."

"I sensed some huge explosions in Mexico City, unnaturally large ones at that. So, that's where we're going. Where shall we teleport to?"

"The Central Cathedral," Lia replied. "It holds monumental worth to Mexicans. So it would definitely be something he'd aim to destroy."

"Then that's where we go." The Three joined arms and were gone.

———•••◦❘◙❘◦•••———

The streets of the Mile-High City were covered in dust and packed with people running for safety, even if they didn't know if or where they would find it. Lucifer was out walking the streets, towering over the crowd as he knocked down buildings, houses, and monuments, laughing at the pain and fear he wrought. Then, a fireball hit the ground in front of him, sending up dirt and dust. He took a step back, then began walking in the direction it had come from. He was lifted off his feet on a gust of wind. Before he could react though, he was knocked off the gust of wind by a powerful stream of water. He was pounded into the ground, where he was engulfed in flames for a few seconds. He however got up with minimal redness on him. "You all still think that will work?" he thundered out, his glinting fangs apparent. He turned away from the chapel, yelling to the air, "Do you find this funny?"

"No, this isn't funny," Aria's voice replied.

"And no, we didn't expect it to work," Lia continued.

Lucifer turned around and saw the Three standing in the center of the street, feet firmly planted, muscles slightly tensed, faces straight as arrows. "So, you didn't learn your lesson the first time?" He let out a snicker. "The death of your friend wasn't enough for you? You need me to kill another one, too?"

"*How dare you?!*" Aria screamed as a tear rolled down her face, a gust of wind hitting Lucifer across the face. "He was more valuable than you will ever be."

Lucifer shook the attack off. "Fine, I'll kill you next. That way, you can be with your pathetic excuse for a boyfriend." He raised his right hand and sent a stream of purple flame at her, but Duke took control and deflected it into a building off to the side, a thick cloud of dust rising from the collapse of the building.

"You're going to have to go through me first," Duke retaliated.

"And me," Lia agreed.

"Well," Lucifer remarked, eyebrows raised, "aren't we just a merry band of misfits?" He turned to stare at Duke, his smile faded. "I would kill Duke for betraying me, but he needs to watch his friends die first." He turned then to Lia, his smile returned. "As for Lia, she will be the last one to go before Duke, leaving him that much more torn and vulnerable." He finally turned to Aria, his smile somehow wider. "So, Aria, you have to be next." As he raised his hand, Duke sped up to him and, grabbing the outreached arm, threw him down the street into a parked semi and threw a fireball after him. The truck's explosion shattered the windows in the surrounding buildings. Lucifer walked out wiping a small line of blood from his mouth. "You just don't know when to stop, do you?" he roared, his smile gone.

"I'll never stop!" Duke shouted, lifting the earth from under Lucifer and throwing him into the air. He was then nailed by a stream of fire and began falling, but stopped in midair, floating gently down to the earth, avoiding the onslaught of attacks heading at him. Once he landed, he fanned his hand in front himself, throwing a blade of dark energy into the ground and blowing all three of them into buildings, all of which collapsed on top of them.

"You three can never compare to the awesome power of darkness that lies within me," he stated as he walked to the piles of rubble, the dust cleared by then. "Get up and fight, if you still can." The piles exploded and the Three emerged, cuts and bruises healing as they wiped the blood from their torn clothes. "Now this is more like it," he smirked.

"It's going to take more than that to take us down," Aria replied.

"Oh, will it now?" he remarked, disappearing and reappearing behind Lia, where he smacked her in the back of the head and smashed her into the ground. He reappeared behind Duke, throwing him into a nearby car. This was when both water and fire hit him, sending him flying into the air. He however stopped and merely put his hand up, gathering both attacks before his palm, compressing it into a sphere the size of a golf ball, and throwing it back at Aria. She put up a shield to block it, but the ball broke right through as if the shield were nothing at all. It exploded in her face, sending her through three entire buildings and knocking her unconscious. "Two down, two to go," he muttered, descending back to the ground.

Duke and Lia ran over to the rubble, Duke tossing everything aside. "Aria," he shouted, finding her motionless and bludgeoned, "give us a response! Be alright, please!"

"Is she alive?" Lia asked.

Duke felt for a pulse, thankful to find it. "Yes," Duke replied, "but she's out cold." He looked up, gently setting Aria down. "Where's Lucifer?" He began moving away, but Lia grabbed him.

"What about Aria?"

"Leave her here. We need to occupy Lucifer before he gets to her and finishes her off." Both of them headed back out into the streets, where Lucifer stood, leaning up against a car.

"Could you two have been any slower at saying good-bye to your gal pal?" he taunted, standing up straight again. "Even I didn't take that long when I said fair well to my fellow angels."

"And I'm sure they were just as quick to celebrate you being out of their lives," Lia replied.

"How dare you?" Lucifer hissed. A stream of dark energy erupted from behind her and pushed her right into his outstretched fist.

"Lia!" Duke screamed. A ball of fire exploded in Lucifer's face and sent him into another building as Duke ran to her side. "Lia, say something, anything."

"I'll be alright. Just look out for-" Her sentence remained unfinished, though, Duke being lifted up telekinetically and thrown down the street, the steeple of the chapel falling to the ground as Duke fell through the roof. "Duke!" she screamed. She tried to get up but got pinned down on her stomach by Lucifer's foot.

"Don't even think about it, my dear," he said, glaring down at her, dark fire forming from his right hand, aimed right at her head. "You may have lived a valiant though tainted life, but it ends now." Suddenly, the doors to the chapel burst open and a steel crucifix flew out, nailing Lucifer straight in the face as he turned to see what the noise was. The stream of dark fire went off to the side, nailing the ground five inches from Lia's face, but catching her left arm and ripping the skin right off.

"However, the power of Christ compels me so say the Lord our God begs to differ with you," Duke countered, flying over to Lia's side and kneeling down. "Are you alright?" he whispered as he helped her up.

"I saw my life flashing before my eyes there for a second, and I need to catch my breath, but I'll be okay," she responded.

"Oh my God, your arm!" he exclaimed, looking at the chunk of her arm missing. He quickly took his shirt off and tied it around her wound, cutting off the circulation to her arm.

"I would have healed it," she replied, holding the wrapped arm close to her now.

"I know you would have, but I'd rather not have to deal with two unconscious bodies."

"That won't be much of a problem," came Aria's voice from behind. They looked over and saw her standing there, her eyes and veins glowing viciously. "Get Lia to safety," she ordered, floating up to Duke's side. "I'll take care of Lucifer."

"Aria, no," Duke rebuked, putting a telekinetic hold on Aria. "This is exactly how Virgil met his end. I'm not letting you make the same mistake."

"Duke," she rebuked, glaring down at him and breaking the hold, "I'll be okay."

"No, you won't," Lia countered, standing with her arm still held to her ribcage. "If he can cause this much destruction with merely a few scratches on him, he's too much for just you."

"Lia, just get to safety. I'm only going to hold him up for a few minutes, that's all."

"That's what Virgil said before his pitiful soul got crushed," Lucifer interjected, standing off to the side, enjoying the arguing between friends.

"Shut up!" Duke thundered, holding Lucifer's lips together with his mind. He turned back to Aria. "He can use black magic in ways I dare not imagine."

"Duke, shut *your* face and get Lia to safety!" Aria thundered back.

"No!" he exclaimed.

"*Get out of here!*" she screamed, a gust of wind erupting and knocking down all buildings in a 500-foot radius, blowing everything in an opposing direction. Duke grabbed Lia in midair and flew back in Aria's direction.

Lucifer snapped his fingers while walking towards Aria. Duke stopped and went to the ground when he heard this. "She's mine," Lucifer stated, that grin of his gleaming at Lia and Duke, who now sat kneeling on the ground.

"Why are we stopped?" Lia rebuked. "We need to help her."

"We can't," Duke responded, banging on an invisible wall. "Lucifer put up an impenetrable shield. White, black, and all sorts of magic along with all physical attacks cannot break it. We can't even teleport through it. Only Lucifer can take the shield down. Either that, or Aria has to kill him to have it taken down. So," he paused, his voice softened, "all we can do is wait and see who the one to die will be."

"Oh, that's easy to determine," Lucifer replied.

"Yeah," Aria quickly replied, "it'll be you."

"Oh, will it now?" he taunted, standing with his hands to his sides. "Very well, then. You take the first shot."

Aria half-smiled. "You'll regret those words," she said as a gust of wind sent him bouncing around the semispherical shield, crashing full force into the ground, the roof, the sides, everywhere. This went on for a few seconds, finally ending with a massive slam into the ground, where a twister drilled a hole through Lucifer's back and chest.

Once that was done, he got up, a hole in his chest, cuts and bruises up and down his body, clothes torn, soaked in his own blood. His eyes gleamed at Aria, rage boiling within him at her surprising strength. As he regained his footing, he pointed a long black claw at her, wounds healing, and shouted, "That will be the last time you will lay a hand on me." A stream of black fire erupted at Aria, who threw up a shield and flew into the stream, slamming him in his torso. On impact, he flew back-first into the shield, but as he fell to the ground, she grabbed him by the hair and slammed his face into the shield, the vibrations of it cracking the black and white magic shields around Aria.

Once Lucifer had fallen to the ground, motionless, Aria's eyes went back to their usual view. She looked over at Duke and Lia. "Did I do it?" she inquired, walking towards them, kneeling down at the edge of the shield, looking at Lia's partially-healed arm.

Duke banged on the dome. "The shield's still up," Duke replied. "So, he's not even unconscious." This was when he noticed motion out of the corner of his eye. "*Look out*!" he yelled, pointing in Lucifer's direction.

Sure enough, Lucifer was getting up, his wounds healing. "Enough of this game," he spat just loud enough for them to hear him. A small ring flew from his outstretched hand, encircling her neck and sinking into her skin. Lucifer looked over at Duke and Lia, pulling the shield down. "You may have put up a fair fight, but I still win. Have fun cleaning her off yourselves, if you even survive." He descended through a pool of darkness, the shield dissipating as he sank.

Aria turned to Duke now, worry across her face. "What has he done to me?"

Duke let out a sigh, tears in his eyes. "That ring will soon build pressure in your veins, and when your veins explode, a wave of dark fire will also explode from you."

"Oh my God," she whimpered, falling to her knees, hands on her head and heart. "I can feel pressure building already. Can't you counter it somehow?"

"Only by transferring it to myself or Lia," Duke replied, almost crying now. He walked over to her, forming a burning blade in his hand, and knelt by her side. "This will make your powers mind, save you from any further pain, and preserve your body."

A tear rolled down her face as she nodded. "I understand." Looking up at him, she smiled. "There is no sin in love, and I know it to be out of love you do this." She pulled him over and hugged him, whispering in his ear, "I forgive you."

"I'm sorry," he still whispered back in her ear before running the blade through her heart, feeling her fall limp within his arms. He then lowered her to the ground and laid her flat before he backed away to where Lia was kneeling. "I never wanted any of this to happen, but fate obviously says otherwise." He put up a shield and both he and Lia watched in horror, tears in their eyes, as out of Aria's body exploded into the sky a stream of dark fire.

As the dark fire dissipated, she and Duke walked over to Aria's body, Lia falling to her knees and grabbing Aria's cold hand, her gaze locked onto her friend's obliterated remains. "Can you heal her?" Lia asked, already knowing the answer.

"No," he murmured, failing to hold back his sobs. He looked down at the torn body, his own tears falling down on the wound. "You shall not have died in vain, sweet Aria." He placed his hand over her lifeless form, absorbing her into himself and gaining the mark of the dragon. Nothing was left of her now besides her memories. "Let's go home," he whispered, standing up and walking away. Lia followed close behind, where she found him in the backyard, setting up a statue next to Virgil's, candles set around the base and Aria's name carved into the base.

"In two days' time, we've had two friends taken from us," Lia stated through heavy sobs. Tears poured down her face. "I say we stop fighting," she remarked after a few moments of silence, looking at all the lit candles and remembering all of the past three years and almost four months they had shared together.

Duke looked at her, disbelieving she just said that. "Lia, after all we've done to get to this point, we can't give up. Plus, this is just two deaths."

"How can you say that?" She started throwing punches and slaps at Duke.

Catching the punches and holding her still, he looked firmly into her eyes, his tears drying up. "Lia, they meant a lot to me. They meant just as much to me as they did to you, I'm sure. They were two of the only true friends I have ever had. However, would you prefer it'd been the thousands of other deaths possible if we hadn't stepped in?"

A few long moments passed, Lia soon responding with, "I know, but I don't want to fight anymore. If you die, I know I can't defeat Lucifer on my own. If I die, there's no guarantee you'll win. Either way, we all lose. So, we need to quit fighting. We can stay here; safe from Lucifer. We can tell Artaxerxes to find someone else."

"Sweetheart, I too wish we didn't have to fight. I too wish those two hadn't died. I too wish we were not where we are. However, fate controls what we do."

"We will still live, though, allowing for Lucifer and Artaxerxes to fight one another in this eternal battle. It sounds like Artaxerxes would end up fighting Lucifer anyway. So, why not just get right to it?"

Duke looked at her deeply, amazed at how much sense that actually made. However, he didn't admit to his amazement. He merely turned and said, "Come on. Let's attempt to sleep. I have a feeling Lucifer will want to play again tomorrow."

"Let's hope this play date is the last of them," she remarked as they walked up the hill and into the house, the Sun setting once more behind the hills to the west.

SIX FEET DOWN UNDER

Duke and Lia were awake late into the night, sitting on the couches in the family room and listening to the silence that filled the house in place of their friends. "Do you think we can do it?" Lia asked, breaking the silence and turning her head to make eye contact with Duke.

"Well," he replied, looking down and letting out a slight sigh, then looking over into Lia's gleaming eyes, "I don't know." He looked back down. "The greater of two powers is fated to succeed, that's for sure. I can't say which side is stronger, though."

"Fair enough." She moved over to his couch and sat down next to him, wrapping her arms around his chest, Duke wrapping his around her. "I just wish Fate didn't have to exist."

"Don't we all?" He held her slightly tighter now. A silence fell between them, Duke breaking it with, "I've thought about what you said earlier, and let's do it."

"Wait," Lia said, looking up at him now, "what are we going to do?"

"I've thought about not fighting anymore, and I say we take a day off. You and I can go somewhere for a day, relax, enjoy each other's company, and have our 'Day of Remembrance' in a way." He then looked down at her, a slight smile across his face. "What do you say?"

She broke free of his grip and stood up. "I say Artaxerxes is going to reprimand us and I was crazy to suggest it. We have to fight, and *you* made that very clear." She was frowning intensely at this point.

"Honestly, to Hell with Artaxerxes." He stood up, throwing his arms in the air. "Even deities need a day of relaxation. He created the Sabbath, did He not? We should get one, too, to recollect ourselves and maybe strategize on how to put an end to this, once and for all. Once that day is done, we'll go back to fighting Lucifer again. We just need one day of no worries what-so-ever."

"Well," she mumbled, looking away and obviously thinking about it, her frown faded, "okay. Let's do it," she smiled, "but just for a day." She looked over at him, holding up an index finger and frowning again. "Where will we go?"

He smiled back at her as he sat back down. "I'm free for anywhere you want to go." He pulled her back onto the couch and kissed her on the cheek.

"Well," she said, obviously giving it some serious thought, "I've always wanted to see Sydney and the Great Barrier Reef."

He snickered. "Of course you'd pick somewhere with a lot of water."

"Hey!" she said, whacking him with a pillow, laughing for the first time in days. "What's that supposed to mean?"

"Nothing," he said, leaning in and kissing her on the cheek a second time. "Honestly, it sounds good. Shouldn't we get some sleep first, though?"

"Since neither of us *can* sleep, we can try, but whether or not we actually will is yet to be seen." So, both of them headed back up to their rooms, attempting round two of sleep.

The Sun shone down on the wondrous city of Sydney, the waters clear and gently flowing in, the winds gently blowing through the trees and over the streets. Duke and Lia walked the streets in their hoodies, enjoying the day as much as they could.

As they walked out into the streets from an animal shelter, they heard a large explosion, followed quickly by screaming coming from down the street. They quickly turned and saw mass amounts of people running over each other towards them. "What the heck?" Duke asked, taking to the air. He looked down the street and saw something he had hoped not to see. "Oh, for Christ's sake!" He waved Lia up to him and pointed down the street towards the eight-foot body standing with his back to them over bodies of residents and visitors alike.

"Are you kidding me?" she spat, letting out a heavy sigh. "So much for our day off." She followed Duke to a nearby rooftop, where they knelt down, watching as buildings fell to the ground and dust clouded the streets. "What are we going to do?" she pressed.

"We're going to fight," Duke answered, sounding dismayed. "As much as I too was hoping for a day off, it looks like it'll have to wait. So, let's finish this, once and for all." He rubbed his chin for a few seconds as he plotted their attack plan. "Okay," he whispered, "you teleport to the roof of that corner building." He pointed to a building past where Lucifer was standing. "I'm going to teleport down to the street and turn him around, so he doesn't see you. Then, you pin him down with jets of water. I'll try using fire, wind, and earth all at once, see if we can end it."

"Are you sure that's going to work?" she commented, thinking such an attack would just annoy him.

"I don't know, but it's better than nothing. Plus, it'll temporarily keep him from destroying the city and give the civilians long enough to escape. If this doesn't work, we fight like we've never fought before. Now, go to that building, but stay low. I'll see you in a few seconds." He gave her a kiss before she teleported away. He teleported to the street below, Lucifer's tall, muscular figure still facing away from him. "Hey, pea-brain, I'm over here!" he shouted.

"Is that the best you have?" Lucifer remarked as he turned, a smirk across his face. The smirk grew wider as he saw Duke was alone. "Do you mean to tell me you're attempting to take me on by yourself? What about your beloved Lia? Has she fallen victim to her own depression?" This was when fifteen or so jets of water sprang from the ocean and pinned him to the ground.

"No, I'm right here," she responded, reappearing by Lucifer as her streams of water were combined with streams of fire, downward gusts, and the earth beneath him turning to diamond spikes. "It's time *you* get washed out to sea, though."

"A) That's a terrible pun, and B) if only that were true," he commented, lifting himself up with no effort, deflecting the pressures off of him. "So much for that plan. What are you going to do now?"

"We'll think of something," Lia affirmed, teleporting to Duke's side.

"You're going to have to try harder than 'We'll think of something' to defeat me," he taunted.

"Then we'll try harder," Duke challenged. "We can still give you a run for your money."

"Oh, can you now?" he taunted. "Somehow, I doubt that, even if you had the powers of the Four *and* Artaxerxes."

A light seemed to appear in Lia's eyes, and Duke noticed the metaphorical light bulb. She however shook her head, as if it was a bad idea. So, Duke let it go instead of asking about it. A rogue wave came up and slammed into Lucifer. Knocked to the ground, another wave then lifted him up and threw him down the street through the windows of a building. The building then exploded in a blazing inferno, crumbling to the ground in a matter of seconds. Lucifer however exited the pile with no more than a bloody nose, which quickly dried up and got wiped away. "You never learn, do you?" he pressed, merely waving a hand and sending both Lia and Duke into buildings, debris falling on top of them. "You start your attacks the same way every time. This grows boring for me. Not to mention that it always ends with one of you dying. Don't you grow tired of this foolish game?"

"No," Duke responded, pushing the debris out of the way and stepping onto the street once more, followed closely by Lia. "This isn't a game to us. This is our life's purpose, and we plan to fulfill it, no matter what the cost."

Lucifer laughed. "You two are so pitiful," he remarked, "still thinking your purpose in life is to take me down. You were merely created to stop me, not to kill me."

"If you're dead, you're stopped," Lia remarked. "Plus, we won't have to stop you again. So, our destiny *is* to take your life."

"Oh, shut up, you know-it-all," he spat, merely snapping his fingers. Duke threw up a hand and put shields around her, Lucifer's attack failing as a result. "You really are beginning to pester me, Duke," he hissed. "It was fun in the beginning to have someone who could counter my powers, but now it's just annoying. Maybe I won't save you for last. Maybe I'll just kill you now." He teleported behind Duke and smacked him across the back of his skull, punching Lia in the face as she flew in for the attack. "It's time to end this."

"Not quite," Lia said, slamming Lucifer in the stomach with her fist and sending him skidding across the pavement. "We've learned how to fight you better as time's progressed."

"Oh, we shall see," he replied, getting up, his back scraped up. He teleported behind Duke and, with a snap of the fingers, Duke fell to the ground. "Now, with that pest out of the way, I can take you out."

Lia ran over to Duke's side, her eyes beginning to glow blue. "What did you do to him?"

"Relax," he said, walking away. "He's just unconscious. Knowing his level of power, he'll be conscious again in a minute or so. However," he continued as he turned back around, "by the time that happens, you and I will be in another part of town, leaving him to find you in the hopes of helping you. However, all he will find is your mangled corpse, torn to shreds by my awesome power." Grabbing her by the arm, he teleported Lia and himself to another part of the city that was as yet untouched.

She pulled her arm away from him. "You say you're so powerful, but you've abandoned the battles after you kill just one of us. Afraid you're too weak to kill a second one?" She watched as her taunting, much to her surprise, took effect. "Then again, it could be cowardice, or both. Whichever it is, it's pitiful."

He glared at her, his rage growing, but the glare and the gritted fangs subsided. "Very well, then," he said. "I had planned on just killing you quickly, saving you any pain and leaving your corpse to be found by Duke once he gets here. However, you seem to want to slow the battle down, suffer longer and make Duke suffer even more as he *watches* you die. So, I'll kill you slowly, letting Duke arrive here just in time to see the final blow get cast." Without hesitation, a dark fire stream erupted from his hand, meeting with a shield of water Lia quickly threw up, holding back the fire for just enough time for a stream of water to hit Lucifer in the back and nail him to the ground. This left Lia the opportunity to fly over and kick him in the face as hard as she could. Her kick lifted him off the ground, and she teleported into the air, where she punched him in the stomach and sent him flying towards the earth. This teleportation-attack strategy went on for almost a minute, each time hitting him in a different body part and each time sending him flying in another direction, all before he could react.

Once he had fallen to the ground, Lia teleported just out of his reach and glared down at his bruised body. "Have we had enough yet, or need I continue?" This was when he took hold of her telekinetically and threw her through four buildings, all of them falling to the ground.

"I'm just getting started," he replied, standing up and wiping the blood from his arms and face. He walked over to the rubble and dug her out, picking her up by the hair and throwing her across the street, glass raining down upon the ground.

She got up, blood running down her face, saying, "As am I." She teleported behind Lucifer to round-house kick him in the face, but he caught her foot and slammed her face-first through the corner of a brick building, breaking her nose. She however took advantage of his hold on her and flung him up in the air, teleporting above him and forcing him down into the ground, the sound echoing off the buildings.

He pushed her off him and, glaring at her, hissed through gritted teeth, "That's it! I'm done with this playtime!" He smacked her with the heal of his hand, engulfing her from every direction in streams of dark fire, pinning her in place. Her shields shattered within the first second, the onslaught hitting her full-force.

"*Stop it!*" Duke yelled, knocking Lucifer off his feet as he flew in, thereby stopping the dark fire barrage. He ran over to Lia's body, still twitching with the remnants of her strength. "Lia, talk to me," he whispered, tears in his eyes. "Tell me you'll be alright." He heard her take a raspy breath, but took that as a sign she was still alive. "Oh, thank God," he cried, putting his arms around her. "You're still alive. Thank God!" He looked into her eyes, tears building in his.

"I wasn't strong enough," she murmured, opening her eyes as wide as she could, the blue illumination faded. "I couldn't hold him off long enough."

"No, Lia," he breathed, starting to cry. "You'll be alright. You'll live. I know you will. I'll take you home, and you can rest. You'll recover, I know you will."

"Duke," she whispered, straining to talk, "it's too late for me."

"Lia, stop talking like that. You're going to make it, okay?" He wrapped his arms tightly around her again, the tears pouring down his face mixing with the blood pouring down hers.

"Lucifer will die by your hand, I know it," she whispered, "but you must have more than the power of four to do it."

"No, he'll die by both of our hands. You'll be there by my side when he falls. We can tell our children about it. We'll live happily ever after, just like in the movies."

"Just remember, I love you, and I always will," she whispered in his ear as she fell unconscious, her body falling limp in his arms, her breathing now labored.

"No," he cried, laying the body down softly. "This can't be happening." He looked down at the motionless body of his eternal love. He stood up and turned to Lucifer, rage boiling within him as it never had before, his eye glowing brighter than they ever had. "You've hurt your last person, you bastard!" As he stretched out his hand, a stream of dark fire five feet in diameter erupted from his hand, nailing a surprised Lucifer square in the chest, instantly shattering the shields around him, relentlessly thrashing his body. Lucifer however managed to put up a hand after a minute and deflected it off to the side, blood covering his injured body.

"Impressive," he gasped, spitting blood on the ground. "You may have been close to killing me, but you won't be given that opportunity again." He disappeared into a pool of darkness, like he always did.

Duke turned back to the motionless body behind him. Tears still in his eye, he fell to his knees by her side. He placed a hand on her face, kissing her lips one last time before standing up. "A warrior's death for the greatest warrior I've ever known." He floated into the air, hands glowing as he engulfed her in flames. As she burned, she turned to solid energy that snaked its way up the streams of fire into Duke, forever a part of him, the mark of the Leviathan finding a new home on his forearm. He fell back to the ground, hand outstretched to where

Lia had just laid. "I truly am alone now," he murmured as he teleported back home. He made a memorial for her, sitting and staring at his new mark, overwhelmed with yet more knowledge, until the Sun had been gone for some time. He then went back up to the family room, where he sat on the hearth and cried himself to sleep.

XXVI

RETRIBUTION

In the course of three days, Duke had lost what truly were the three closest friends he ever had. He, however, was not going to let them die in vain, or even die permanently if he could help it. He spent the next morning searching through what knowledge he had for a way to bring them back, but it didn't work. So, he got up from the hearth where he had been laying, began pacing around the room, and saw the List sitting on the table. As he looked at it, it glistened at him, almost like it was trying to tell him something. He picked it up, and all the letters changed to English this time, as if it recognized him as the god of all four elements now.. That was when he saw it: a fifth line revealing itself at the bottom. He read it: "To fulfill your destiny, you must release your full potential." The image of Lia's "lightbulb" earlier flashed before him, and he now understood what she said with her dying breath. He dropped the paper back on the table, realizing what this meant. *Artaxerxes must have limited our potential when He first revealed Himself to us so we wouldn't pose a threat to Him when He came to kill us Himself. We never stood a chance against Lucifer! Well, no more!* He flew out the back door and high into the clouds, summoning all the power within him, and, eye glowing, he noticed what felt like restraints within him. So, he gritted his teeth and pushed against them, veins glowing as he felt himself pulled back towards the ground. So, he pushed harder and harder. He began to groan, and then yell out, pushing against the veritable "glass ceiling." By now, he had touched down on the yard behind the house, every muscle in him now clenched as he struggled to stand up. *Just a little . . . longer . . .*, he thought, giving one last push with everything he had within him. That's when he felt the glass ceiling shatter, rocketing into the air and out into space, time seeming to stand still and the icy darkness all around him becoming light.

With the restraints broken, he felt his head start throbbing with yet more information and his muscles building greatly as not only he came to his full-potential, but the powers of the others within came to full-potential as well. His skin burned as the markings of the gods changed on his very skin. The phoenix and the dragon both opened their wings to cover his shoulder blades and chest respectively. The Leviathan on his left forearm opened its mighty jaws, and the tigress on his right forearm went from a sitting position to a mid-run position.

After the light faded, he looked around, his head no longer hurting, but somehow aware of the whole earth at the back of his mind. Time had seemingly unfrozen due to his loss of concentration. Thinking it best to get some fresh air in light of what just happened, he landed in the backyard again where he proceeded to stumble down to the memorials, panting as he fell at their bases. The candles flickered in the gentle wind, the sunlight fading as the Sun met the horizon. He looked up at the statues. *I have failed you, my friends.* He clenched his fist. *Not again, though. Now, I avenge the days our lives were betrayed, both by the darkness* and *by the light.*

"Duke," he heard Artaxerxes call out as He floated down to the monuments, standing then next to Duke, "what troubles you, my son?"

Duke tried to hide his frustration with Him as best as he could. "The only real friends I ever had are dead, and I can't help but feel betrayed," he said, his fists clenched.

"But you *have* been betrayed," Artaxerxes responded, laying a hand on Duke's shoulder. "Lucifer has betrayed your life by taking away the lives of those you hold close. That is why you must go out and defeat him. Avenge them, my son!"

"I will, but first, I have something else to take care of." Duke immediately whipped to his side and lifted Artaxerxes off the ground with one hand. "First, you owe me an explanation for *why* you limited the powers of all *four* of us. You make us go up against your failed attempt at an archangel, but you do so after hindering our powers. What hope did we have then of succeeding in the mission you gave us?" He slightly tightened his grip on the Lord's neck.

"Duke," He implored, grasping at Duke's hand, "put me down, now."

"Not until you tell me *why*."

"Fine, fine. Put me down, and I'll tell you." Duke hesitantly obeyed, setting the Deity of Light on the ground. "Releasing beings of such power as I knew you would become into this world was too dangerous, especially having a human side as the four of you do. I either risked the world getting destroyed by Lucifer upon your failure or the world getting destroyed when such awesome power was brought against those who have wronged you, which is essentially the whole world. If you all died fighting Lucifer, though, I could finish the task in your stead, keeping the world safe."

"Darkness cannot exist without light, nor light without darkness, though," Duke replied. "The deities of the elements knew this, so how is it you don't?"

He let out a sigh. "You are right. Darkness and light are always fighting one another, always present with the other. Should Lucifer fall, another darkness will arise in his place."

"Like the one in the void?" Artaxerxes twitched in surprise, and Duke noticed. "It's not just a dream then, and you *do* know about it."

"Of course I know about it, but I'm curious how *you* know."

"Dante knew-"

"-and when you absorbed him, you gained that knowledge."

"Yes." Duke cracked his neck and stared down the god. "You're not completely light though, are you?" He smiled, coming to a realization about the deity. "No, I think you have a little darkness within yourself, just as Lucifer probably has some light within him. That tiniest shred of light would account for his only taking one of us at a time and his letting me be the one to absorb them into myself. That tiniest shred of darkness within you accounts for your fear of our power, fear of the destruction we might cause if released into the world unrestrained."

"Silence!" He spat. "How dare you speak to me in such a way?" He threw a ball of light at Duke, who threw up a shield and deflected it.

Duke started taking a step towards Him, Artaxerxes starting to back up. "You were afraid we'd overpower you if you took us on otherwise. Four on one, and the odds would be in our favor."

"Okay, fine, yes. When the original spirits were put to sleep, I limited their powers in case they were resurrected. Is that what you want, to know you're right?"

"No, I don't want, nor do I need, that affirmation. What I want is to avenge those three." He pointed to the statues with the candles lit. "They were betrayed by Lucifer *and* you. So, I will find Lucifer eventually and put that fight to an end, win or lose, just as you have ordered and for which I have been born. You'll get your wish. However, you betrayed them as well by ensuring their doom, meaning you must meet the same fate as your fallen son."

"Don't call him that!" Artaxerxes cried. "He's not my son! I don't know him, and I don't want him!"

Duke twitched in a sudden rage as memories of his own father came rushing back to him. "You're just like him, my father." His eye began to glow. "You cast aside your own child because he caused problems, condemned him to a life in Hell, and didn't look back on your decision . . . how did I not see this before?"

Realizing what was about to happen, Artaxerxes threw up a shield. "Duke, think about what you're about to do. Do you really want to be remembered for this, for killing God?"

"Oh, you wouldn't really die." Duke raised his eyebrows. "I'd absorb you into me. Your knowledge would become my knowledge, your powers my powers, your strength my strength. Lucifer wouldn't stand a chance, then. It's just as Lia said before she died. It takes more than the power of four to defeat Lucifer, and that's what I intend on using."

Artaxerxes let out another sigh, seeing He would have to win this battle the hard way. "Very well," He said, standing defensively. "You leave me no choice."

"Bring it," Duke replied, hurtling a stream of fire at Artaxerxes. It met with His shield and pushed Him back into the trees. Pushing back with a wave of light, He summoned trees to form all around

Duke, imprisoning him in an area no larger than his body. That didn't hold him, though, as Duke teleported out and punched Him in the face. Artaxerxes fell to the ground with a bloody nose and Duke went to stomp on Him, but He reacted, disappearing and putting Duke in a choke hold. Duke broke the grip after a couple seconds, throwing Artaxerxes over his shoulders and skidding across the ground. Diamond spikes flew up threw His hands and legs, holding Him in place. He teleported off the spikes, though, quickly healing His wounds and flying at Duke, fist at the ready. Duke caught the fist, the sound of the impact echoing and shaking the trees around them. Duke pulled Him into a choke hold and locked His arm behind Him. "Give up yet?"

"Never," He replied, struggling to break the hold, though He ended up having to teleport away, reappearing behind Duke and slamming him across the back of the head. Duke fell to the ground and, upon rolling onto his back, blasted Artaxerxes in the face with flames, burning the collar of His robe. Artaxerxes dropped the smoldering robe, His muscular chest now apparent. Duke flew at Him, fist at the ready, but He caught his fist, needing two hands to hold it back. Free to do so, Duke used his other hand to punch Him in the chest, the shields around Him shattering.

"Time to end this," Duke commented. Before Artaxerxes could react, a stream of dark fire pierced through His body from behind and went into the earth in front of Him. Falling to the ground, terribly weakened, He held up His hands as if to surrender. "What? You're giving up?" Duke asked.

"Duke," He replied, "believe it or not, I don't want to fight you." He looked into Duke's eye. "I understand your anger, and you have made nothing but valid points tonight. You and I both know that you will win eventually, just as we both know you're not merciless enough to kill in cold blood, at least not anymore." This gave pause to Duke. Seeing the glowing in Duke's eye subside, He smiled. "You are not the man you once were by any extent of the imagination. You took me on, not knowing if you'd win, knowing that many would call you 'heretic' or 'heathen' for such actions, but knowing it was the right thing to do." He stood up, weak in the legs and holding His chest. "Such dedication to those you love, such leadership skills, such strength of will . . . Perhaps people will see me as 'weak' or 'not-so-omnipotent' for this, but all that matters is that you understand. You defeated me, fair and square, and given that I have come to the end of life yet again, it falls on me to find a successor. Suffice it to say, you have proven yourself truly worthy of my powers, of taking my place as God and having my knowledge. Here," He said, holding out His free wrist, a scar on it Duke had never noticed before. "If you wish to end me and use my powers to end Lucifer, do what you must." There was a twinkle in His eye, a tear of joy rolling down His cheek.

Duke stood frozen in place, not truly comprehending until now that, if he did this, he would *be* God. He let out a deep breath, disbelieving this was real. "Are . . . are you sure . . . master?"

Artaxerxes began tearing more at being called "master" one last time. "Yes," He replied, "without a doubt in my mind." He patted Duke on the shoulder, smiling. "If this is what it will take to put an end to Lucifer and to finally find peace, do what you must." Fighting through the moment's hesitation, Duke grabbed His wrist. As He began to turn to energy, He said, "Live well, my son," the voice echoing into the distance. He then flowed into Duke. All the power and knowledge of Artaxerxes fused with Duke, ending with the mark of God appearing on His left hand: a dove carrying an olive branch. After that, somehow unaffected by the massive influx of power and energy, Duke touched the ground around Him, sending away the summoned trees and fixing the damage done in His battle. He then continued to stare off into space, thinking of nothing but His friends and the task at hand, realizing it wasn't even in God's power to return the lost to life once gone for so long.

After a few hours of sitting there, He stood up, somehow unaffected by the even larger amount of knowledge that had flown into Him, feeling enlightened and ready for the task at hand. "Time to get Lucifer," He declared as He went inside. Sitting in a trance, He finally sensed at the Vatican a great distress. He sensed purple flames emanating from the ground and some of the surrounding buildings. "That's my cue," He said, summoning a white cloak and pulling the hood up. He didn't know what would result from the battle, but He knew that this would determine the fate of the Universe.

So began the final battle.

XXVII

DESECRATION OF HOLINESS

The Vatican, one of the holiest sites in Christianity, stood in chaos. The fountain at the center of St. Peter's Square had been toppled, as had a few of the pillars around the square. Hundreds of people ran screaming away from Lucifer's giant form while multiple ranks of clergy ran out with holy water and Bibles in hand; some to try and exorcise the deity, some to perform expedient last rights for those who had been killed in the few moments since Lucifer had shown himself. Not realizing he was the actual Devil and not just possessed by him, the works of the former were soon found to be of no use. They were swept off their feet once they got close enough, many not making it through their rough landing. Dark fire erupted from his hands, sending the surrounding city up in flames.

The Pope finally came rushing out. "Please, my son," he beseeched, slowing his pace as he approached Lucifer, "why do you lay waste to our Father's creation?"

"I am not under your God's jurisdiction, puny mortal." Lucifer backhanded the Pope, sending him skidding across the ground, unconscious. "You however can save yourself by abandoning your God for me."

"Satan be gone!" many cried as they surrounded the Pope. Sensing the fear and pain within so many of the people around the Pope, Lucifer raised his hand to immerse the holy man and all those around him in dark fire.

"*Halt!*" a voice from behind them thundered. The flame dissipated as both looked to see a figure in white robes floating down from among the statues, a white aura about Him. "You have done enough damage for one day, Lucifer." The figure landed on the ground by the Pope, hands hidden inside the robe's sleeves. He threw up a shield in front of them and told the crowd, "Let me through that I might heal him." Kneeling down by the Pope's side, He laid a hand on his forehead, healing the injuries within him and bringing him back. "You can go, Your Holiness," He stated, looking down upon the Pope. "Tell everyone to get inside and stay there. I will deal with the demon myself."

"God bless you in this battle, my child," the Pope declared, running back towards the cathedral and waving others to follow as Duke dropped the shield.

"You can't play God forever, Artaxerxes," Lucifer stated, not knowing the figure was actually Duke. He released a stream of dark fire on the figure, who merely put up a hand and allowed the fire and energy to build in front of Him. After a minute of building, Lucifer ceased his attack and watched as all the dark fire he had just released upon the hooded figure condensed until it was no larger than the size of a bullet.

Duke wrapped His hand around the bullet, feeding fire, water, wind, earth, and light energy into it without Lucifer knowing. He walked towards the Devil a few more steps, saying, "You will have to do better than that." He flicked the bullet at Lucifer. It hit him square in the chest, where, upon exploding, it both shattered Lucifer's shields and blew a hole right through the deity. "Besides, I am not playing," Duke replied, pulling His hood down. "Your Father has ceased to be, and I have absorbed Him, thereby becoming Him."

Lucifer looked at Him for a moment, disbelief written across his face. "You killed Artaxerxes?" he finally repeated, healing himself as best as he could and reestablishing his shields. "Fine, I'll play along with whatever game this is."

"This is no game. He betrayed the Four as much as you have betrayed us. Therefore, having both released the full potential of the Four and having become Him, I will do to you as I did to Him. Once I take your life, I will absorb your very being into myself, never using those powers for anything but good."

Lucifer ran his hand through his hair, snickering at the thought. "Dark powers used for good? Hah, such a kidder." The smile faded from his face after he realized Duke was serious. "Fight me all you like, Duke. You will never get as close to taking my life as you did the other day."

"We shall see about that." A stream of fire erupted from Duke's hand. Lucifer stood there, thinking he could take it, but he couldn't. The stream hit Lucifer full-force and sent him flying backwards, skidding across the ground and into a fallen pillar, which broke in half upon impact.

"You're stronger than I expected," he commented as he got up, the back of his shirt torn, wiping blood from his mouth. "You really must have killed Him . . . maybe this *will* finally pose a challenge for me." He disappeared, reappearing to Duke's side and attempting a punch across the face, but Duke dodged and punched Lucifer in the stomach, Lucifer falling back from the impact. He walked up to Lucifer and lifted him up by the front of the shirt, slamming him right back into the ground.

"You are making this too easy."

"Am I now?" Lucifer pressed, getting up, blood running from his nose. "Take this, then." Eight streams of dark fire engulfed Duke where He stood, nailing Him from every direction. After it was done, Duke fell to the ground, motionless, all but His pants burned off, blood running down His arms, neck and back. "I'd say this isn't easy for you at all." Lucifer went to stomp on Duke's spine, but Duke rolled out of the way, dark energy erupting from His hand and knocking Lucifer over.

"Correct," Duke replied, wounds healed in an instant. "This will not be easy for me, but then again, I wasn't expecting 'easy.'" Duke disappeared and reappeared to roundhouse kick Lucifer in the face. Lucifer however caught Duke's leg and threw Him through a pillar, which broke in half. Duke, however, flipped and rebounded off the pillar behind it, flew back out, grabbed Lucifer by the hair, and threw him into the air. He reappeared above Lucifer and kicked him back into the ground, flying down to nail him in the stomach. Lucifer disappeared at the last second, though, reappearing at Duke's side and kicking Him in the side, sending Him flying and skidding across the pavement into the fountain. Lucifer then reappeared behind Duke and kneed Him in the back, Duke flying through the air but disappearing before He hit the ground.

When He didn't reappear, Lucifer looked around for any sign of Him, but there was none. "Come out, come out, wherever you are," he teased, continuing unsuccessfully to find Duke. He suddenly fell into a hole that appeared below him. Lucifer was then forced down by a strong gust, surrounded by water and liquid metal, and then buried by millions of pounds of earth. The water started boiling him alive as he began punching through the hardened earth above him.

"I'm right here," Duke called, floating ten feet in the air, as Lucifer burst through the ground, soaking wet and burnt. "I was here all along."

"You think you're so funny, don't you?" he hissed, throwing excess water everywhere and healing his burns.

"No, but I had fun doing it," Duke replied, a smile across His face. "Did you not have fun during your little swim?"

"No," he replied, "but I will have fun hanging your head on my wall."

"I would like to see you try." Duke disappeared and reappeared, attempting to punch Lucifer in the chest, but Lucifer grabbed a hold of Him, slammed Him into the ground a bunch of times, and finally stomped on Duke's back, the sound of Duke's back cracking echoing off the pillars that still remained. As he went for the second stomp, Duke disappeared, reappearing about 20' away, His pants soaked in blood, but fully healed. "You missed me," He taunted. "Even after you've wounded me, you still can't hit me. And I thought your *army* was weak. So much for that thought."

"What was that?" Lucifer yelled, rage building within him. "Did you just say my minions were stronger than me?"

"Well, at least we know your hearing is good." He tapped His cheek with a finger as if attempting to figure something out. "It is unfortunate your strength has suffered, though."

"That's it, you traitorous rat!" he thundered, eyes gleaming brightly. He threw a thick stream of dark fire at Duke, who then threw one of His own in return. The two streams collided part-way between them, each of them pushing against the other, the energy building up in the center. It began to form a ball of solid dark fire, glowing brighter as it grew larger. It grew to about fifteen feet in diameter, where it reached its limit and exploded. While knocking down what remained of the colonnade, it sent Lucifer and Duke skidding across the ground. A crater 100' in diameter now rested between them, both of them resting just beyond the edge.

As Lucifer got up, he looked over to see Duke doing the same. "Never have I been opposed by such a force as you, even when I was against the original Four. Then again, never again shall I." Lucifer's eyes began to glow purple.

Duke looked over and saw this, His own eye beginning to glow. "I second the notion," He replied, the smile gone from His face. "No more fooling around, Lucifer. This ends now."

"I thought you'd never ask," he said, flying right at Duke, who ducked out of the way and elbowed Lucifer into the ground. He then kicked him into the air and sent a stream of dark energy into Lucifer. Lucifer however took that energy, formed it into an attack of his own, and sent it right back at Duke. Duke however put up a hand, the ball of energy teleporting and nailing Lucifer in the face, sending him through the rubble behind him. He got up and summoned another stream of dark fire to hit Duke, this time from behind. It hit Him square in the back and sent Him hurtling toward the ground. Just before He hit, He teleported out of sight again. Lucifer flew over to where Duke had fallen, but He was nowhere to be found. "Come out, coward!" he shouted. Duke reappeared at the edge of the crater. "I knew you wouldn't chicken out on me," Lucifer called as he flew at Him, punching and kicking Duke repeatedly, but this didn't last for long. Duke soon blocked a punch and reversed the attack, now laying an onslaught of His own kicks and punches upon Lucifer, the shields around Lucifer shattering. Duke snapped His fingers, disabling Lucifer's powers if only for a moment. Lucifer tried throwing a dark fire ball at Duke, but nothing happened. He stood up straight, brushing himself off. "You may have disabled my magic, Duke, but I don't need it to defeat you. I can tell you are closer to death than I am. It will just be a few minutes now before you'll be with your friends."

"Oh will it now?" Duke retorted, quickly flying in and punching Lucifer in the stomach as hard as He possibly could. Lucifer flew back and slammed into the toppled statue from the fountain, the shields around him breaking. "I beg to differ." He flew up to Lucifer and pinned him to the ground. He then leaned over, snapping His fingers and knocking Lucifer temporarily unconscious. Duke, realizing He only had seconds to do this, teleported Lucifer into the center of the crater, teleported Himself into the air, and, with every ounce of energy He could muster, summoned forth a stream of dark fire 20' in diameter, infusing it with fire, water, wind, earth, and light. It erupted out of both hands and encased Lucifer's body, pushing him further and further into the ground. Lucifer regained consciousness just a second too late to react, therein feeling the full pain of the attack. Unable to move or do anything, he did the only thing he could manage: let out a horrible scream.

After a few minutes of pure onslaught, Duke let up the attack and descended to Lucifer's side, the body twitching at the bottom of a massive hole. "How did you do that?" Lucifer whispered, amazed at what had happened.

"How are you still alive?" Duke countered, looking down at the almost-dead deity before Him. "That should have killed you."

"I never expected to die," he murmured, attempting to stand up, but only to fall back onto the ground, "let alone by the hand of someone so insignificant and pitiful as you. I was mistaken." He looked directly at Duke now, his eyes returned to the regular red glow, staring deep into His eyes. "You are the greater power of the two of us. Your determination, your strength, your compassion, it all amounted to becoming something greater than anything even I could overcome. Congratulations, Duke Edward Vulcous. You have defeated me. I wish you luck in your now-meaningless life." Lucifer's eyes went blank, his body falling limp on the ground, lifeless.

Lucifer, the Deity of Darkness, the fallen archangel and son of Artaxerxes Himself, was now and forever dead.

Seeing that the Deity of Darkness was no more, He walked up to the lifeless form, placed His hand over it and turned him to pure energy, which then flowed into and became a part of Duke. He looked down and noticed, along with the increased power and knowledge, the mark Dante had given Him had changed. No longer was it a skull. Now, it was a raven with a rose.

Realizing the humans above were waiting for reassurance of it being safe, Duke created a second white robe and put it on, flying up to the field of destruction that remained. "It is safe to come out," He boomed, watching as the people came out of hiding.

The Pope eventually made his way out and stood before Him. "My son, what is your name?"

Duke looked at the ground, thinking about this question intently. Rather than answer, He snapped His fingers, regenerating everything that had just been destroyed to its rightful place and condition. He then looked back at his Holiness. "I am known by many names. You know me best as Elohim, Jehovah, and Adonai."

"My Lord," the Pope gasped, wide-eyed and quickly prostrating himself, the thunderstruck crowd following suit, "I should have known it was you who would save us all."

"Rise, my children," Duke commanded, watching as they did so and smiling beneath His hood. "Hear my words: You have all been blessed with the gift of life this day. Thousands among you within the last week all over the world have not had that opportunity. Therefore, as I leave you, I command all of you to not forget to cherish what life has brought and is yet to bring you, no matter how simple it may be. Every day is a blessing and is to be cherished as such." Duke teleported out of sight, hearing the crowd breaking out into prayer and hymn as He did.

Once back at the house, He flopped down on the couch. *My work is not done yet,* He thought to Himself. *Now, the* true *final battle begins, but first, a good night's rest.* Duke closed His eye and fell asleep almost immediately.

XXVIII

MAKING AMENDS

The next day arrived, and with the rising of the Sun came Duke, arising to a challenge of a different sort: making amends for the damage done over time. Before He left, though, He stepped out to the memorials out back, placing His hand on each of the statues. *You all are here with me, I know*, He thought, *but that does not change the fact that I still have a human heart that misses and mourns your losses.* A tear rolled down His face. Not knowing what else to do, He summoned three roses and placed them on the bases of the statues. *Time to make amends*, He thought as He disappeared from the house.

⸺∘°∘❈∘°∘⸺

Grosse Ile, MI; a land destroyed by the temper of a yet-untrained hothead. The ashen ground lay lifeless, the air eerily absent of the sound or presence of life, the woods all over the island nothing more than smoldered remains. One of many police boats ran up and down the river, making sure no one tried sneaking onto the desolate island. Duke appeared on the water halfway between the wasteland and Canada and began walking on the water towards the island.

"Hey, freeze!" the cop in the boat shouted, not knowing whether or not he was hallucinating. Duke ignored him though, continuing to walk on the water to the island and continuing to ignore the shouts of the cop in the boat. Once He arrived, He knelt down and laid a hand upon the shore. A wave of light shot across the island in all directions. The ash disappeared as grass began to rapidly grow in its place. Trees sprouted to life and the sound of all sorts of creatures began echoing through the air. Last but most certainly not least, though not at first seen, near the renewed town hall, there rose from the ground a large stone. In the stone was engraved the words "In Memory of the Fallen" and plaques of those who perished in the fire embedded in the stone below it. "Well, I'll be," the cop commented, scratching his head in disbelief. "Hey, son," he called out. Finally acknowledging the officer, Duke stood up and walked over to the boat. The officer reached out and laid a hand on His shoulder. "Okay, so I'm not dreaming or hallucinating, which means-" He pointed at the island, unable to finish his sentence.

"Which means that Grosse Ile is now a livable township of Metro-Detroit, that people can move back there, attend school there, play golf there, and go shopping on the one street of business on the whole island."

The officer quickly hopped on his radio. "Umm . . . Officer McNichols to all other officers patrolling the waters around the island, are you all seeing what I'm seeing?"

"Affirmative, Officer McNichols," came a voice over the radio. "Requesting clarification on how to proceed."

"Um . . ." He paused for a few moments before replying, "Open the bridges. I repeat, open the bridges, and send word to headquarters." He looked to Duke and asked, "Who are you?"

"I'm no one of importance," Duke replied. "I lived here once, and I wanted others to live in the same safe community I grew up in." Before the officer could say another word, Duke disappeared.

Meanwhile, some thousand miles away, the workers and politicians of Maine's capital building were beginning to arrive for another day of work. They walked by the memorial to the victims of the Maine Hurricane every day, a reminder to all of the lives lost on the most unfortunate of days. Sitting at the center of the roundabout in front of the state capital building, all that was left to remember the fallen was a plaque on a misshapen rock and a small flower bed, something the senators and representatives had been fighting over how to build upon for years. This day, though, was different. On this day, they saw a figure in a white robe standing in front of the monument, looking as if it were paying homage to the victims. Many stopped and looked, pointing and talking about who this mysterious person might be, some saying they recognized Him as the one who saved the world the day before, but no one knowing for sure. Pretty soon, the whole front of the building was covered in people, and the security guards were dispatched to break up the crowd. Seeing the source of the problem, one of them approached Duke, baton drawn. "Hey, buddy, you need to move. You're causing a hold-up to those needing to get to work."

Duke looked up at him, then back at the monument. "A friend of mine lost family on that fateful day. I was just hoping to figure out a way to fix the damage done to help her feel at peace." He looked up at the capital building and the surrounding neighborhood, seeing it had been rebuilt. "It looks like everything has been repaired, though."

"Unless you can bring the dead back to life," the guard replied as he put his baton away, though not removing his hand from its hilt, "no can do."

Duke lifted His head. "Well, perhaps there is one thing I can do." Looking at the guard, He said, "You might want to step back, though." Watching as the guard stepped back, Duke made a lifting motion with His hand. Then, out of the ground erupted a 25' statue of Aria's mother and father with one hand around each other and the other saluting. Around the top of the marble base were the words "Remember Our Fallen Leaders." The rest of the base below was covered with plaques of the names, dates of birth, and positions of all those who had died that day. Around the base then was a one-foot ring of snapdragons, Aria's favorite flower. This filled the roundabout from edge to edge, and the watching crowd stood flabbergasted at what they had just witnessed. "Yes, I think that will bring her peace," He commented, "just as it will put to rest the negative thoughts of the politicians and workers who walk by it every day, thinking such a momentous tragedy deserves far more than a rock and a few flowers." Before anyone could comment, He disappeared, moving on to His next place as the crowd He left erupted in applause and cheering.

⸺∘∘⊶❈⊷∘∘⸺

The next stop on Duke's "Tour of Redemption" was Lia's birthplace in Indiana. As He appeared in the small town in the northeast quadrant of the state, Lia's memories of this place flooded over Him as if they were His own, filling Him with the pain she had long felt as an outcast of the church her mother and grandmother attended. This then was amplified by the distaste Artaxerxes had secretly felt for such cultic "churches" as this.

He landed in the parking lot across the street from a small, sandy brick building. The steeple was missing and the bell tower looked to have been damaged by many rainy seasons. The lights from the sanctuary shown through the giant stained glass windows on the side of the building. Seeing this building He Himself had never seen except through Lia's eyes, and having the knowledge of other things they had done and said through Artaxerxes' watchful eyes, a renewed rage flowed through His veins. *It's time they learned what it is to follow Christ*, He thought to Himself. He willed smoke to form underneath all the smoke detectors in the building, setting them off and sending the congregation sprinting out the doors. Seeing Him there and recognizing Him as the one who saved the world only a day earlier, they ran to Him, prostrating themselves and beginning to say the Lord's Prayer, Psalm 23, and singing a wide array of hymns.

"Get up, and silence your hollow praises!" He barked, rising into the air as He blacked out the Sun with storm clouds and giant lightning strikes.

Confused, they arose, though fearful and tensed. They looked at each other, hoping someone else might have an answer as to what was so upsetting. Seeing much the same expressions on every face they saw, they eventually all turned to a bald man in his mid-70s with glasses and a suit. He stepped forward, and in his raspy voice, said, "My Lord, I don't understand. We are your most-devoted followers, doing all that you command. What have we done to so displease you?"

"Pastor Screech," Duke boomed, "you and your church have done a great *many* things that are displeasing to me." He lowered Himself back to the ground, His hood still concealing His face from them. With an upward wave of His hand, He lifted the fragile man into the air. "For years, you have let your God complex get the best of you, judging others for how they live, how they act, and how they speak, never once truly admitting to your own faults. You have cast aside your fellow brothers and sisters at a moment's notice, scorning them, referring to them as 'problems' rather than 'people.' You have been quick to label those that have disagreed with you in any way as 'heretics' and 'heathens.' Never once have you paused to question whether your beliefs were even what the teachings of Jesus Christ taught, whether *your* beliefs were the ones that were irreligious and heretical." He dropped the man to the ground with a thud, the congregants quickly running to help him up and pulling him away from Duke.

"Master, I've merely done-"

"*Silence!*" He bellowed with a resounding echo, eye and scar glowing. "I have heard your lies for far too long and will hear no more of them." He waved His hand and the pastor's vocal chords were frozen in place, instantly muting him. "And you all," Duke continued, turning to the mortified crowd, "you have let yourselves buy into this hateful nature of this, your golden calf." He pointed a flaming finger at the pastor, who cowered in fear, unable to yell out. "Many of you knew that what he said was wrong, that it contradicted the teachings of Jesus, but you remained silent, choosing rather to do what was easy rather than what was right. Where once you were a loving church, caring for all in the community and fighting for what was right, you have now *ceased* working in the community, but rather have let your focus be solely inward, focused only on yourselves. You talk about each other behind one another's backs, never once thinking that perhaps the solution to your qualms is actually talking with one another."

Duke spat fire on the ground before them, causing a minor explosion that sent bits of pavement every which way. "No, this church is no church," He concluded, shaking His head in disappointment. "It has cast aside the teachings of Christ for self-centeredness, self-proclaimed righteousness, and abused Christ's good name to justify its vile words and actions. You all have dug your own graves, and I feel compelled to turn you all to ash where you stand." He heard a gasp from all of them and saw tears begin to fall.

"Please, Lord," the pastor's wife cried out, kneeling beside her husband and holding him against her chest, "show us mercy. The good book teaches us that you are wrathful, yes, but that you are also merciful towards us, your children."

"You are no children of mine," Duke spat. "Such hatred as lies within your hearts marks you as devil spawn, not children of God, and I cast you all aside as such." He formed a ball of dark energy in His right hand, raising it above them and watching as they shook with absolute terror. "However, you do have a point," He said in a much calmer voice. The crowd began to loosen a little bit, a feeling of hope spreading through them as they looked to one another. "I am a God of mercy, and therefore, as reparations for your years of Sin and hollow words, I grant you all two options. You may rebuild this church; actually *reading* the Bible and *following* the commandments to love and care for one another; actually *meaning* those words you pray, sing, and preach; and to love your God rather than use His name in vain. Otherwise, you may scatter like cockroaches to other churches in the hopes that you might all learn what it is to love your neighbors, Christians and non-Christians alike, to mean the words you say, and to love your God. Regardless of your choice, I hereby disband this cult and its envenomed meeting site, and I cast it into the hellish depths to which it belongs."

He threw the dark energy across the street, where it landed on the sidewalk and formed a circle around the building. The congregation watched in horror as their hundred-year-old building began to sink into a pool of boiling magma, slowly catching fire and melting into nothing before them. The pool of magma quickly cooled, forming a cylindrical stone slate where just moments earlier, the building stood. Duke heard the sobs of the congregation as this cherished site became nothing more than a grave of sorts. He snapped His fingers and the pastor's vocal chords were unfrozen. "This is the mercy shown to you all this day.

Your options have been given. Choose wisely, for mercy such as this shall not be shown again." Duke disappeared from sight, not even a bit of remorse in His heart for the pain He had just caused.

Duke reappeared in the center of the sink hole that was once Santa Barbara, CA. He looked around, seeing people looking down into the hole as if it were a tourist attraction. He heard them yelling at His appearance, security guards and guides yelling at Him to get out of there because it was a restricted area and unsafe. He ignored them, though, lifting His hands as the earth began to shake. The land began to raise itself, buildings reconstructing themselves and standing back up, streets reforming, pipes reconnecting beneath the ground. The crowd shouted in amazement as the city that until that moment had been destroyed repaired itself.

Once done, they rushed over the barricades into the city, finding Him standing at the center of Alice Keck Park Memorial Garden, standing before a rock much like the one erected on Grosse Ile a few hours earlier. He held up a hand, giving them pause. "The great city of Santa Barbara stands around you once again, and just as before, you are free to live and shop here as you please."

"Who are you?" He heard a small voice in the crowd call out.

Duke looked over to see a small girl holding a teddy bear at the front of the crowd. "I am no one of importance," He replied, smiling. "A friend of mine used to live here, and he recently passed away. He loved this town, and I thought it best to give him back the town he grew up in as a 'going away' gift, if you will." Before anyone could say another word, He disappeared from sight, teleporting to New York City, Mexico City, and Sydney. There, He laid a hand upon the ground with many onlookers standing in awe of what was going on around them. He reassured them He was no one and merely left so as not to create too much of a spectacle.

After a day of making amends for the damage done by the Four and in the final battles, He teleported back to Harbor Springs, MI, standing firmly before the real estate agency Lia's mother ran. Stepping through the door, He merely walked up the stairs to her office, not even stopping to address the receptionist at the front desk, who merely stared, frozen and speechless in disbelief of who just happened to waltz through the door.

Duke knocked on the door to the manager's office, hearing her bustling in there. "Just a minute," He heard. A few moments later, the door opened, and she tripped over her own heels in surprise. He caught her with His powers and lifted her up again. "P-p-p-please! Come in, sir!" She stepped aside and waved Him through. "To what do I owe such an honor? A home for the savior of the world, maybe? We do have some great houses, both for rent and for sale." She quickly ran over to her desk and began searching for papers with different houses' information on them.

Duke stepped through, willed the door shut, hands folded within His sleeves, His face hidden beneath His hood. "I'm afraid I'm not here to ask for a home, Charlotte." He stepped over to the window behind her desk.

She removed her glasses and tilted her head. "Then, something else I can offer you, perhaps?"

"I am here to tell you that your daughter is gone," He said. "She was a colleague of mine, and she fought the same evil as I. She fell to his merciless hands, and I thought you might just want to know."

Charlotte pulled her head back and frowned. "Why are you telling me this?"

"I tell you this because it is only proper to know that one's child is no longer with them, that they died fighting for the good of all persons." He looked over at her. "I know you pretend to hate her, and that you've even convinced yourself after so long that it is true, but if you look deep within yourself, you will find that motherly love overcomes all hatred and resentment."

"I don't love her, though," she quickly replied. "She took away from me my chances at true success. She earned my parents and myself nothing but scorn by our fellow Hoosiers. She is the product of a man I wish only the worst possible death. She comes in here stealing a property from me, a property that I've had to go through all the paperwork of marking as uninhabitable so that no one goes seeking it out. She has brought me nothing but trouble. As far as I'm concerned, good riddens with that waste of air."

He placed a hand on her shoulder. "You tell that to everyone, and you're starting to believe it yourself. Think back, though. Think to the smile on your face when you felt Lia kick for the first time. Think about the tears of joy shed when she was delivered into this world. Think of the joy it brought you to see her smile, to laugh, to ride her bike. Perhaps they were few and far between moments, but there were moments of joy with her as well. You might hate her origins, how others treated you because of her, but she didn't ask for that either. Amidst it all, she loved you, even if you didn't express that same love for her." He removed His hand and began walking towards the door. As He got there, He willed the door open and paused, turning His head towards her. "Whether or not you believe it, she was proud of you, loved you, did what she did in the hopes you might be proud of her." He then faded into a whiff of smoke and sailed out the door before she could respond.

Charlotte stood there, those last words resonating within her. Looking out the window at the sunset, she stood there in silence for a while, time seeming to slow to a stop. Seconds became like hours as she reflected on His words, realizing He was right. With the revelation came a tightening of the chest, a tensing of the muscles, an opening of the floodgates. "Oh, my Lia, my little Ellie Bell, my baby," she whispered, beginning to shake. "No," she began to repeat, every time a little louder until she was shouting it, beating the window, tears flowing like two white rapids. She fell into her chair, head in her arms, weeping.

Charlotte missed her little Lia.

He arrived home, threw off the cloak and stared out upon the sunset. He willed the candles around the bases of the statues to light, illuminating the statues of His friends. *Wherever you are, I hope what I have done today has brought you all peace at last.* He stood out upon the balcony an hour or so more, not knowing what would happen next, then proceeding into the house. There, He turned on the TV, seeing reports all over the news networks of His work that day.

"Many people are flocking back to Grosse Ile to try and buy up property on island, especially along the riverbanks. If you've ever wanted an island home, now's your time."

"The people of California are overjoyed to have the cultural center of Santa Barbara back, both for living and for supporting the economy of the state."

"No longer are the senators and representatives of Maine fighting over how to afford a proper monument for that terrible disaster only a few years ago. Now, they've agreed to move forward on other bills and proposals before them."

"Many churches, big and small, are now feeling the heat and reassessing how 'loving' they are towards each other and their neighbors, fearing their church might face the same fate if they don't shape up."

Eventually, He reached the more conservative news stations, and they were showing the social media messages of the President, claiming all of this was in response to a prayer she said the night before.

So much for this being over, He scoffed.

"The President will be holding a public rally tomorrow in celebration of her success at fixing the terrible deeds of the Four and the disasters from the last few days," the network said.

Then that's where I shall be tomorrow. He turned off the TV and closed His eyes, settling down for what was sure to be an interesting day.

XXIX

THE FINAL TASK

If ever there was a place and time you didn't want to be driving, it was midday in downtown Washington, D.C., much less when the President was holding a rally. Crowds were swarming the streets to see her speak in front of the Capitol, police forces were on high alert, and snipers lined the rooves of the Capitol and the surrounding buildings, which left all the monuments abandoned of tourists. For this reason, Duke appeared on top of the Washington Monument, out of sight, at least for the time being. Looking around, He sensed a tension amidst the snipers on the roofs, sensing their dissatisfaction with having to serve the current president.

The tension among them increased as a portly, middle-age woman in a deep purple skirt, blazer and thick red curls approached the podium on the Capitol steps. The crowd began cheering and whistling as she stepped out. "My fellow Americans," the President began, waving for silence, "I stand before you today as your President, as the most successful President in history." Applause and cheering erupted as she finished just one sentence. "Like the rest of the world, I, too, feared for the safety of our world with the Four running around, causing death and destruction wherever they went. In an attempt to repair their damages, I prayed that God would fix this world and prove once and for all that our country is the greatest country of all." The crowd began to chant "U-S-A," and, smiling, the President motioned for them to settle down. "I said a prayer, and God, in full support of me, answered my prayer, almost as if He were doing my bidding. The death and destruction we have seen in places like New York City are an all-too real reminder that evil is out there, especially such evil as caused by the Four as they run free. Young or old, rich or poor, Black or White, we are all at risk in the face of such danger as those monsters. That is why I am initiating an Executive Order that all Americans have authorization to kill the Four on site along with anyone found supporting them or withholding information as to their whereabouts." At that moment, a force field she didn't know was around her rattled with vibration as bullets attempted to pierce it from all around. She ducked to the ground, covering her head at the sound of gunfire. The crowd began running toward the President to protect her, but they were kept in place by another force field. Realizing the rounds weren't causing harm to her, they all looked around, seeing that it was in fact the Secret Service themselves and the First Gentleman who were firing on the President.

Once their rounds were used up, the crowd began yelling out of anger, and the President started looking around for who had saved her. Seeing Duke floating towards her, she pointed in His direction, continuing, "You see, God fully supports me and condones all my words and actions." The crowd looked up in amazement and watched as He continued to float towards her. "You will hear from the monstrous news that God wouldn't condone my actions, that America hates me, that I am the worst president in history. Look before you now. See how this disproves everything they say, right here, right now. God supports me." The crowd erupted into cheering and whistling yet again, chanting the President's name and "U-S-A" yet again.

"*Silence!*" Duke boomed, landing on the platform. In an instant, the whole crowd fell dead silent. The sky over DC started turning a dark red color, black storm clouds forming and purple lightning cracking but not touching down. "Are you all really so blind to the truth right before your very eyes?!" He called out to the crowd, motioning towards the President. Not a peep was made by all in the crowd. "The First Gentleman has attempted to publicly assassinate his wife, and those sworn to protect the President have all joined him in committing this heinous action. You all want the truth? There is your truth!" He pointed to the pile of bullets surrounding the President.

"Um . . . God," the President began, slowly approaching Him, covering up the microphone, "what are you doing?"

He turned to the President and lifted her into the air by her shirt collar, her hand no longer covering the hot mic, and sewing her mouth shut at a snap of His fingers. "Mrs. President," He boomed, "I didn't save you because I support you. I believe that no one should have their life taken from them before it is their time; *that* is why I saved you. I however do *not* support you, your words, your beliefs, or your actions." He heard a gasp from the crowd. "I've followed what you've done, and to say that what you do and say is 'deplorable and egregious' would be an understatement. Your own husband has tried to kill you, along with the men and women charged to protect you. That alone speaks volumes, but that's not all.

"Your ideologies and actions, your words, as exemplified by your new Executive Order, place you on the same level as such dictators as Hitler. You claim to be Christian, yet nothing you say or do is remotely Christian, nor have you ever even entered a church. You literally are the worst sort of human, perpetuating hatred rather than love and unity. You lie to all your followers, never once sharing the whole truth of what you really think of them, how you mock them behind their backs. No, I did not save you because I approve of you or anything you stand for. I saved you because everyone deserves the chance to come clean, to make amends. Now is your chance, Mrs. President. Do you repent?" He snapped His fingers and the stitches on her mouth came off.

"I repent for nothing because I've done nothing wrong," she replied, "and you are not God. All I say is right and just, and therefore God would approve of me and all that I stand for. You are a fake God." She began to laugh as she heard "Fake God" being chanted behind them. Duke's temper rising, He struck the Capitol Reflecting Pool with purple lightning, water exploding out onto the crowds, but the crowd's chanting was not abated. The President laughed at the crowd's resilience and persistence. "You see, these morons will listen to anything that I say and take it as fact." Suddenly, the crowd fell silent.

"I think they heard you," Duke said, pointing to the hot mic, "and I don't think they appreciate being called 'morons' or being used like that." He looked out over the crowd and saw people, coming to reality on the situation, drawing their guns. "I think they're about ready to kill you." He turned back to her. "Care to repent now that the first true thing you've ever said has been broadcast over live television to the whole country?" He dropped her to the ground, watching as she turned pale and began to shake. "You realize the whole country will now be after you, and I won't be around to protect you. So, make your move."

"Okay, okay, I'll do what you ask," she murmured. "Just save me from them." She pointed out to the crowd, who at this point were chanting "Kill her" and "Down with the president!"

Duke turned to the crowd. *"Silence!"* he bellowed. "Though she is to blame for much of what has happened, you all are just as much to blame." The crowd then fell silent again. "Many of you out there have done terrible things simply because one woman has said it's okay. Never have I seen such despicable behavior from any country besides this one." He turned back to the President. "She is the president who has divided this country so far down the middle that it will be lucky not to enter a second Civil War. Tell me how anything she has said or done is worth supporting, saving, or defending." He paused, but she was left speechless, backed into a corner and unable to lie her way out this time, and the crowd too was speechless.

He turned back to face the crowd again. "You see, no one here can deny the claims I have made." He summoned a screen of water in the air, and on it began to show scenes from the battle between Lucifer and the Four, Three, and Two. "Watch as the ones you all have referred to as 'monsters' fight the same creature I defeated two days ago. Watch how they die trying to save the world from that beast, defending the people who hate them out of fear." He looked out over the crowd, seeing their faces turning white in confusion and astonishment, some holstering their guns while others just dropped them to the ground. "They sacrificed their lives for you all." He turned to the President. "They did it even for you, Mrs. President, and yet you scorn them and hunt them like rabid animals." He looked back out at the crowd one last time. "Look inside yourselves, and assess whether or not *you all* are the animals." He heard a hard gasp from the crowd as their world was turned upside down and they began to see reality for the first time. He turned back to the President one final time. "Given that I am in a good mood, I'm giving you one week to correct *all* the wrongs you have done. Make no mistake, though, that should you fail to correct even one misstep *in its entirety*, bad reviews from the media and public slander from those who don't support you will be *nothing* in comparison to the wrath you will face from me." He disappeared from sight, hearing and feeling the astonishment within the crowd.

AN UNINVITED GUEST

When Duke got home, He sat down before the monuments, wondering whether He should be feeling remorse for His actions, and after some time, determined that what He did was justified. She was another demon who was in need of vanquishing, and He did what He could to properly dispose of her lies and misdeeds. He then went up to the house and turned on the TV to CNN to see if His speech had worked. The President was standing before a crowd on the front lawn of the White House. Clearing her throat, she said, "My fellow Americans, by now you have probably seen the divine intervention that happened earlier today. In response to that, I have a few actions in place of the one I was going to enact earlier. First, I have written up an Executive Order that will disband all concentration camps currently holding our nation's Muslims prisoner." Duke noticed her dissatisfaction in doing so, let alone saying it, but somehow felt glee in seeing her pain. "Next, in light of their actions, their bravery, and their service to not just our country but to our world, I now pardon Duke Edward Vulcous, Eleanor Cordelia Neptuosa, Virgil Spencer Adams, and Aria Rose Harmos, known to many as 'the Four,' of all charges against them and order their records expunged." She physically gagged, looking physically ill at this point. "Third, I will be releasing all financial records, tapes, emails, and documents that may have any holding on the charges brought against me to the appropriate authorities that, in good faith, if I have in fact committed any wrongdoing, I may be charged for my crimes by our wonderful judicial system." She was absolutely pale at this point. "Lastly, I will be stepping down as President at the end of this week, that I may be charged for any crimes I may have knowingly or unknowingly committed, and leaving this nation in more capable hands than my own." She paused, hands clenched tight on the podium as if to hold herself up. "Thank you," she finally managed, stepping down from the podium. Cameras began flashing brighter and more rapidly than usual at what was sure to be a most-historical event.

Only one thing left to do, then, He thought, smiling as He turned off the TV. He went to step out onto the back balcony, but as He reached for the handle, there was a knock at the door. He paused, sensing who it was and clenched His fist before stepping out onto the back deck and willing the front door open with a gust of wind.

Through the door stepped a man in his mid-50s, his light red hair neatly combed to the side, his polo and khakis covering heavily-burned arms and legs. "Hello?" he called, walking deeper into the house and looking around until he saw Duke on the back deck. Quietly, he stepped through the open door onto the deck, saying, "I was wondering if I would get the chance to talk to you."

Duke let out a sigh, hands clenched tight around the railings. "You survived; impressive," Duke said. "Now I at least can have closure."

"I'm just as surprised as you are that I survived, son," the man said, smiling a little.

"I'm not your son," Duke spat, hands clenching the railing tighter. "You would have to have been a father for me to be your son, and you were by no means a father."

"I know," the man replied. "I was a horrible father. I don't deserve that title in the slightest. I deserve to be dead, to have been consumed by your rage all those years ago, but somehow, I'm alive. I don't know how, but I am. Call it an 'act of God' or a chance at setting things right."

The railings began to snap under the pressure. "I'd ask how you found me, but honestly, I couldn't give less of a damn. What I really want to know is why you're here, Ed," He said, teeth gritted.

"I'm here to talk, that's all." Ed held up a hand defensively, seeing Duke was obviously and understandably not pleased to see him. "I just want to talk, and mostly to tell you . . ." He paused, hands starting to shake. "To tell you that I'm sorry," he finally finished, "for everything."

"You're sorry?" Duke repeated, His hands crushing the railing as He tried to maintain control. "That's all you have to say? You're sorry?" Duke looked over at His father, eye and scar glowing. "You show up at my house after all this time, neatly dressed and somehow alive, whipping out some cliché apology, and I'm expected to just say that everything is fine, that all's forgiven? I don't think so." He threw a fireball at a tree down the hill, and it exploded into a thousand sharp splinters. "You're dead to me, just as you have been for four years."

"I'm dead to me, too," Ed replied. "If you'll just calm down and hear me out, I'm sure you can find it in your heart to forgive me."

Duke clenched His fist, fire engulfing it, Ed holding up his hands further in defense. Seeing the fear in His father's eyes, He unclenched His fist and pointed towards the family room. "You get one chance." He entered the family room and sat down on the hearth, Ed close behind, plopping down on the couch across the room from Duke. "Start talking," Duke barked, glaring at Ed.

"I woke up in a hospital a few days after your accident," Ed began. "I don't really remember much of that night, or at least, I didn't at first. Bits and pieces have come back to me with time, but mostly your rage, and your pain, which instilled in me guilt beyond anything I knew possible. Per the doctor's orders, I wasn't allowed to drink, which, as you might understand, sent me into withdrawal, which is another story for another time. Regardless, I was put on heavy pain killers as I learned to walk again and as the skin grafts covering all but my face healed. The doctor said that, because I covered my face with my arms, that I only suffered minor burns to my head and neck in comparison to the rest of me. He got me hooked up with a local Alcoholics Anonymous group that I've been seeing ever since. I've been sober now for over four years." He pulled a purple medallion with gold around the edges out of his pocket and tossed it over to Duke. "This Twelve-Step program has turned my life around, and I've been able to make amends with everyone except for you," Ed continued. "For that reason, I haven't let them move me to the next step, because I haven't made amends with the one person with whom I truly need to make amends, and that's you."

"So, what you're saying is you came here so you can move on, like this never happened?" He tossed the coin back to His father.

"Duke, I was the worst sort of father that ever was, and I realize that now." He let out a sigh. "After I lost your mother, I took all my grief and anger at the situation out on you, and you deserved so much better." A tear started rolling down his face. "I can't undo what I've done, and trust me, if I could, I would. I would take back every punch I threw, every shot I took, every hurtful word I said. I want nothing more than to start over with you, but I know I can't." He sobbed a little before continuing. "I fully admit that I don't deserve your forgiveness, but I cannot fully forgive myself until I know I have your forgiveness. Please understand that I've come so far from who I used to be. I'm a changed man, and I will do whatever I can to make it up to you. What would you have me do, son? Name it, and I'll do it."

Duke stared at Ed in silence for a few minutes, eventually letting out a sigh. "You're right, you don't deserve my forgiveness. In all truth, you deserve to burn for everything that you did to me, all the pain you caused." He lifted His hands and flames began to emanate from them. "You deserve to be turned to ash right here, right now, like you should have been four years ago."

"Then do it," Ed said, standing up and opening his arms wide. "Turn me to ashes if that is what it will take." He stared at Duke, actually smiling, saying, "Do what you have to do, because I love you, son."

Duke paused, the flames dying. "What did you say?"

"I said, 'I love you,'" Ed repeated, letting his arms fall. "I know I don't deserve your love in return, but you remind me so much of her, of your mother, of the woman I fell in love with way back in the 9th grade. She had a fiery temper about her, too, just like you, and Lord only knows it got her in some tough spots."

Duke paused, staring off into space as He stepped out onto the back deck again, feeling a strange feeling in His heart. He felt all those years of hatred washing away, replaced with empathy and love for this man. Ed followed, standing next to Him and staring off into the distance with Him. "You really are sorry, aren't you?" Duke finally asked after a half hour of silence.

Ed looked over at Him. "Yes, I am, and I've wanted to tell you that so badly for the better part of four years now." He smiled. "What do you say, son? Can you forgive this old windbag of his past life?"

Duke's head fell, and He shook it before lifting it again. "Yes, I can . . . and I do." He looked over at His dad and smiled. "I forgive you, Dad."

Ed began to cry, wrapping his arms around Duke. "You have no idea how much that means to me."

Duke tapped Ed's hands before saying, "This is the last time you can see me, though."

Ed pulled away. "But, we can fix our relationship. We can start over, be a real father and son, do all the things fathers and sons should do together."

"No, we can't," Duke replied, the smile fading from His face as He looked away. "They were right to lock the four of us away. Our powers make us a danger to society, and just because we saved the world doesn't mean everyone has forgiven us. Yours and my being related makes you a target for those who may still want to get to me." He sighed. "You need to leave and not tell anyone that we are related. That's what you can do to make it up to me: go away, and don't come looking for me again."

"Ah," Ed replied, eyes averting to the ground, "I see." He looked back up at Duke and placed his hand on His shoulder, half smiling. "I understand, and I thank you for your concern." He wrapped his arms around Duke tightly, saying, "I will miss you, son, more than words can say."

"I know," Duke replied, "and I will mourn not being able to reconcile our relationship more, but it has to be this way." He turned and wrapped His arms tightly around His father, letting go after a few moments. "Go, be safe, and know that you are forgiven for your past sins."

"Thank you," Ed said, wiping a tear from his eye as he walked back through the house and out the door, closing the door behind him.

Duke let out a sigh, feeling both relieved to know His father would be safe, happy that His father's blood was not on His hands, but sad that He had to turn down the opportunity to get to know His father anew to keep him safe. He shook His head, telling Himself, *It has to be this way.* He waved His hands over the railing, repairing the damage He had just inflicted upon it. Then, He stepped out onto the back lawn and lifted the house with the rest of the surrounding land off of the ground and into the sky until it was surrounded by nothing but clouds. He commanded the river to circle around the floating island so it was always flowing. He then ordered the monuments to go to the other side of the river, resting near the edge of the landmass on their own piece of land. Finally, He commanded each to be inscribed with the message "Died fighting for a better tomorrow. May the stars shine down upon their souls, wherever they may be. May they rest in peace. May they never be forgotten." He walked to the right of the memorials and sat down, watching the Sun set across the massive sea of clouds. He soon fell asleep, His head up against Lia's memorial stone.

So began a new life for Duke.

EPILOGUE

Oh how the time has passed since those most unfortunate days. It is strange I should be writing about them, since they were both some of the worst of my life and, oddly enough, they are not the whole story. In fact, this is only the beginning, as the events of this story happened also in three different places, where Good and Evil came to one final clash, all leading to a far more intense battle here in our Universe. I'll get to that a little later, though.

Regardless, from that time, Duke began to feel immeasurable relief, as if the world were no longer pulling down on His soul, at least for a time. Immediately following the fall of the President, He made sure to visit the monuments every day, laying roses by them out of what was sure to be eternal pain. Even as God, He missed His companions with all of His being. As much as He missed them, though, He finally concluded that resurrecting them was beyond even His abilities, and therefore, constantly mourning their loss would only hurt Him for all eternity.

As for life on Earth, the USA returned to a balanced state, or as balanced as it could be anyway. Religion became more prominent both because of humanity's knowledge of His existence and the words He spoke. They have started to love neighbors as equals, to question the consequences of every word and action, and have been made all the better for it.

This was not the end of Duke's journey though, nor was this the end to Evil's reign.